Bury the Past

Copyright © 2024 Jane Phillips

Published by The Peapod Press

All rights reserved. No part of this book may be reproduced in any form, or by any electronic or mechanical means – except for the inclusion of brief quotations in articles or reviews – without written permission from the author.

ISBN: 9798300544508
Cover photo © 2023 Jane Phillips
Cover design © 2024 Amy Phillips
First edition 2024

This is a work of fiction. Names, characters, places and events are products of the author's imagination. Any resemblance to actual persons, living or dead, is purely coincidental.

Books in The Burials Series

Bury the Truth

Bury the Lies

Bury the Pain

Bury the Past

Mary

Mary said we could.

So:

Be more Mary!

Acknowledgements

Book Four is the last book in the 'trilogy'. It's been a long haul to get the last one out as there were so many loose ends to tie. I can thank the same people again for still being there. Well, mostly! A very special thanks must go to my amazing sister, Mary, and my erstwhile writing friend, Fraser, both of whom have thrown off this mortal coil far, far too early. I miss them!

My City University friends, Vicki Bradley, Paul Durston and Vicki Jones have been with me for the long haul. Glyn, my partner in life, (but not in crime) has been with me for over fifty years. He and our two lovely daughters, Amy and Sian, have helped me just by being there. Kai, Melody, Max and Leo are our future and are truly wonderful. Amy stars again as my Very High Priestess of On-line Anything and Glyn continues to make strong dark tea.

About the author

Jane Phillips is a psychologist. This gives her an unhealthy interest in the criminal mind. To counterbalance, she has a husband, two children and four grandchildren. They do their best to keep her on the straight and narrow but she is determined to grow old disgracefully – so, watch out world!

Chapter 1

Tuesday 1ˢᵗ October 2013

'That's two now. They're picking off the low hanging fruit first.' Henry pointed to the Births, Marriages and Deaths section in the local paper.

Katy read out the short piece, two lines only. 'On 29ᵗʰ September, Sir James Hutchinson, 87, died peacefully in his sleep at The Hollies rest home. Funeral details to follow.' She flicked the paper. 'Could just be a coincidence. How old was the first one?'

'He was 89 but he was in rude health – or so my informant tells me. Played golf every day. He choked on a boiled sweet two weeks ago. We know they were both in Murdock's conspiracy video. That's too much of a coincidence for me. Ben, I think you should inform Parker. MI5 need to know.'

Ben looked up from his paper. 'You sure? The main plotters are dead. Surely that means the plot is dead. Why would anyone want to kill the others? It doesn't make sense. They weren't integral, just useful. They're old and sidelined and are probably relieved that they've been let off the hook.'

Henry waved his stick around before replying. 'It only makes sense if the IRA has found out about them and is systematically killing them. If that's the case, then the entire plot has been uncovered and all our good work could be for nothing. Yes, there are only two so far, but murder just smells right. Understand that?'

Ben nodded. He knew the feeling; for him it was a tingling in his fingers that told him something needed to be investigated.

Katy looked thoughtfully at Ben. 'Still, Dad. Best to. Just in case, eh?

'Let's see what Mary says.'

Mary poked her head around the door. 'See what Mary says about what?'

Katy laughed. 'Were you earwigging? Henry's smelling a

rat and we want to know if his nose is OK.'

Ben explained the outline of Henry's argument with several interruptions from Henry. Mary listened intently then said, 'If I remember rightly, there were ten, maybe twelve, plotters on that video. Murdock and Knatchbull are dead and they were the leaders. MI5 has told us that the others have all been identified and have had the fear of God put into them to stop them stepping out of line. We know the plot was to kill the entire Catholic population of Northern Ireland so, if the IRA is now systematically killing the plotters, they must know about the plot and we have an enormous problem on our hands. We know who the plotters were and we've been told that that there was an Enforcer but we've no idea who that person is or was. There was that army type whose torso appears in the video but not his head. We need to check that MI5 has found him. So, yes, we need to see Parker.'

* * *

Within ten minutes of Ben's phonecall, a car had arrived to whisk the four of them to Millbank. When they got to MI5 headquarters, they were shown into the self-same room in which they had handed over the evidence of Stanley Murdock's plot to commit genocide in Northern Ireland. For Ben, it brought again the realisation of the huge implications of the task they had accomplished, and the repercussions if the job was still not finished.

As usual, Parker was flanked by three anonymous grey men. He came straight to the point. 'So you think Hutchinson's and Braybrook's deaths are related. Any evidence?'

Henry replied, 'Smells wrong. One of them was fit as a fiddle, the other rickety, I'll grant you. Died within a fortnight of each other. Needs investigating.'

'Agreed.' Parker turned to Ben. 'We need to ensure that this plot is put to bed once and for all. Since your call, I've arranged for you to bury Hutchinson. Fortunately, he's not too far from your usual territory. You're good at winkling out intel that others miss. See what you can find out from his erstwhile friends. I've also arranged for a post mortem. Your usual fellow will do it. Mustn't raise too much dust. I'll send someone to liaise, in case he needs extra resources. Braybrook's been cremated so no confirmation to be had there.' He paused. 'What do you need?'

Ben replied, 'Contact details for Hutchinson's next-of-kin and contact details for the other conspirators, some background on the other conspirators, a copy of the recording of the meeting they all attended. That should do for now.'

'Details, yes. There are no next-of-kin. He was the last of his line. Can't let you have a copy of the recording. That recording will never leave this building. You can view it here whenever you need to.'

The grey suits nodded. Ben had known he would meet resistance. That video was dynamite because, if it fell into the wrong hands, the Good Friday Agreement would be in tatters. He saw the point and decided they would have to be content with viewing on-site if needed.

Katy added, 'We need a copy of the covering letter that came with the evidence.'

Ben had no idea why his daughter wanted that letter but he trusted her instincts. 'Yes, thanks Katy, of course we need that letter.' He noted that Henry, who appeared to be asleep, nodded and smiled at this request. Parker looked to either side and the suits shook their heads.

Katy tried again. 'It really belongs to my dad as the finder of Murdock's incriminating stash. It was addressed to him. He needn't have handed it over to you.'

Mary joined in. 'Let's put our cards on the table. If these men have been murdered, someone has found out about the plot. My first instinct is IRA or an offshoot. We need to act fast. If Katy says we need that letter, we need that letter.'

Parker turned to the man on his left. 'Get me a copy and I'll have a look at it. And details of the conspirators.' The man excused himself and left the room. 'If that is all, I'd like to move on to other matters.'

Ben held up his hand. 'Before we move on, the man in army uniform in the video, have you ascertained who he is?'

'Not yet. Difficult, that one. No clues, no insignias, just his torso in a khaki uniform. And Murdock didn't mention him in any of the paperwork you gave us. Still working on it. We'll let you

7

know when we crack it. Now, moving on to another set of mysterious people, the photographs that came in Murdock's box. We are no nearer to finding out who they are.' He slid copies of the four photos across the table. 'We could do with your help.'

Henry laughed. 'So we can take these ones away, I suppose?'

Parker looked sheepish. 'Henry, you of all people know how we work. We keep secrets unless it's in our interest to divulge them. It's in our interests to let you have copies of these photographs. If you can identify these four men, it would be extraordinarily helpful.'

Ben picked up the photos and examined them. There was nothing on the back and, on the front, the mug shots of four men with menacing expressions. These faces said to him, 'We are not to be trifled with.' Ben was sure he wouldn't 'trifle' if he could possibly help it. He placed the photos in his inside pocket. The grey man reappeared and handed the copy letter to Parker. Parker glanced at the contents then passed it across the table. 'Some of this should be redacted but I'm taking responsibility for its inclusion in the text going to you. I'm sure it will be in safe hands. I hope this too will be in our interests.'

Henry chuckled. 'Of course. Of course.' And Ben saw Henry give a surreptitious wink in Parker's direction.

Parker gave a half smile and then looked straight at Ben. 'I'm afraid we've rather neglected Northern Ireland recently. Thought it was all tied up and that ship had sailed. Henry's been keeping us updated on the situation in Eastern Europe and it's been exercising all our minds here.' He added quietly, as if to himself, 'If not the minds of our masters.' He shook his head. 'Anyway, it seems we need your help in another matter related to Ulster. We have an assignment we wish you to undertake and you are the only person who can perform this particular task. We want you to talk to Jeremiah Knatchbull.'

Ben laughed. 'But he's dead! I'm not a medium, you know.'

'Ah, yes, of course. The world thinks he's dead. We decided it would be expedient for his death to be announced. In our interests, so to speak. He's not dead, he's still incarcerated. He won't talk to any of us and he wants to see you.'

Chapter 2

As soon as they'd returned and were settled in Ben's kitchen, Katy said, 'Read out Murdock's letter. I know it will tell us something.'

Mary picked it up and started to read. *'If you are reading this, then our plan to rid the North of taigs has failed. We got some of them but the Fenian lovers in England will have won this time.'*

Katy interrupted. 'No, no, skip to the last paragraph.'

'But he doesn't know where these are; no-one knows. Even our Enforcer doesn't know. So how the hell did you find them? This will not end. The cake gets demolished and then there were Neele and the Colonel. No matter – but be warned. This battle's over but the war goes on. No surrender.'

'See, that sentence has always bugged me, even before we handed it over to the spooks. It makes no sense and the tenses are all wrong. We know Murdock was a stickler for correct usage. Henry's lecturer friend, you know, the one that taught Murdock, well he said that Stanley would never use poor grammar. He was adamant about that so there must be a reason. And who are Neele and the Colonel? They're not on that list of conspirators. Hang on, I'll google it.' They waited as Katy tapped into her phone. 'Agatha Christie? What's she got to do with all of this? Sorry folks. I'll love you and leave you. I've got to go and read up on Agatha.'

When Katy had left the room, Henry smiled indulgently. 'She's wonderful, isn't she. Next week, starting at Ethel's. Big wrench, eh? Don't worry, I'll keep an eye out from afar. She won't even know that this old dodderer is watching over her.'

Ben smiled. His younger daughter was leaving home, off to study at his old college. A few years ago he'd have been terrified for her safety. Now he could consider his reaction to be that of a normal parent, a mite worried but also excited for her and the opportunity that student life would present. He knew he had two women to thank for his continuing recovery from the burden of PTSD, his therapist, Alison Clare, and his soulmate, Mary Amelina. He silently thanked them both.

Henry continued, 'Mary, read out the paragraph about the election.'

'I thought I'd settled it when I made sure that bloody interfering woman was killed. But she must have got a message through. They foiled us. Our man within couldn't stop them getting Blair elected. Pathetic. Outflanked by his own people. Someone in there knew – someone skewed the election. Never found out who.

'Ben, this tells us that your wife must have got through to HQ to warn them of the plot. But we don't know who she got through to. Parker knows. My bet is that it was him but we'll never be able to prove it – and why would we want to? The change of government in '97 foiled the plot then and we've foiled it for now. But we don't know, with these killings, who is seeking revenge. Or, more importantly, what will be the outcome'

Mary patted the old man's arm. 'Henry, we don't even know yet if it was murder.'

'Of course it was murder.' Henry replied. 'When's the PM? That'll confirm it.'

'Tomorrow morning. I'm going to walk over to see Jim Spire immediately he's finished.' He smiled at Henry. 'Should I tell you the result as soon as I know or should I keep you in suspense?' He didn't wait for an answer but pointed to the clock. 'First though, my visit to that other dead man, and this dead man will want to talk to me. He said he'd talk to me and only me. Intriguing!'

Chapter 3

Before setting out on his visit to Jeremiah Knatchbull, Ben looked again at Murdock's letter. Murdock's evaluation of Knatchbull gave him hope that he could get something useful from him – if he played it right. He read again the section of the letter that mentioned Knatchbull by name.

Knatchbull is a lightweight. True to the cause but none too bright. He's been a useful shield but, without me, he'll eventually go under. He'll crack under pressure so I've only told him what he needs to know.

Ben was pretty sure that Knatchbull had been 'our man within' mentioned in a previous paragraph but that was not certain. There was the possibility that two moles had co-existed within the Services. If that were the case, one could still be there. The allusion to Knatchbull's lack of intellect, Ben felt could be taken with a pinch of salt. He had it on good authority that Murdock had been exceptionally intelligent as well as arrogant, so would probably have deemed anyone below genius level to be a lightweight. It remained to be seen whether Knatchbull would crack under pressure, for pressure was not what Ben was going to use. He was going to use guile. He was sure there was a great deal to be found out, if Knatchbull could only be persuaded to part with his knowledge.

* * *

Checkpoints and a forest lay behind him; the prison and its two armed guards before him. Ben decided that he was being fanciful in believing that the forest had grown since he'd last attended this man's call. That had been in the summer when the trees had been in full leaf. He had no idea what the trees were but their leaves were now turning a uniform muddy brown. Between that and this, his second visit, Knatchbull's obituary had appeared in all of the broadsheets. As he was searched and his identification scanned, Ben wondered if Knatchbull would be kept here, imprisoned alone, like Hess, for the rest of his life. Rudolph Hess had been tried and sentenced. Jeremiah Knatchbull had not been granted a trial or any means of protesting what might be mitigating circumstances. If there were to be a possibility of Knatchbull being reprieved, then exploring mitigating circumstances might be a way of getting some truth out of him. That was one avenue Ben might follow.

* * *

'Hello Jerry. You're looking good.'

Knatchbull was indeed looking well-cared-for. He still wore formal clothes, a suit and regimental tie with a handkerchief standing erect in his breast pocket. His brogues were polished to gleaming and the crease in his trousers was sharp. His jacket was unbuttoned. At first glance, Ben thought he had put on weight, but further examination suggested that he had been working out and had become more muscular.

'Hello Ben. Good of you to come.' Knatchbull held out his hand and Ben shook it. The guard made no objection. Knatchbull turned to the guard, 'You can leave us. But could you rustle up some tea and those nice biscuits?'

The man nodded and withdrew.

Ben opened the dialogue. 'You said you wanted to see me again. So I came. What can I do for you?'

'Not much, old boy, except keep me alive.'

'Ah! So I'm to be the conduit for you to dribble bits of information out to those who might decide that you are expendable.'

'Precisely. Don't misunderstand. I'm not unhappy here. I've always been a solitary type, a bit of a misanthrope I suppose, so the solitude doesn't really bother me. But one day I hope to be free, and you are my one and only ticket to freedom. If I can survive until they know I'm no danger, I may get my wish.'

'So what have you to tell me?'

'Oh, Ben, slow down. That would be too easy. You must ask

me questions and I will decide whether or not it is in my interests to answer them.'

Ben had to smile at the terminology. Interests – the same thought process as the high-ups at MI5. But, of course, Jeremiah Knatchbull was MI5 deep into his bones. But also a terrorist. 'Let's start with an easy one. The other people in the video I sent you. How deeply involved were they?'

Knatchbull replied, 'Mixed. They were useful. They had contacts in government and beyond. They were all committed to the cause, some more than others.'

'Clever how the person behind the camera made them count themselves in. He gained their commitment and had the evidence to prove it. Makes them ideal blackmail material.'

'Our leader was a very clever man.'

'Last time I saw you, you talked about your leader but you never said who he was, only that he was dead. Can I assume that the person completely out of view was the leader?'

'I think I can give you that.'

'But no name?'

'Now really, Ben, you wouldn't expect that.'

'OK, but I have to try. Give me a few crumbs. The one in army uniform. I assume he's the Enforcer. What about him?'

'No, you can't assume that. And you'll have to decide when I'm telling the truth because I have been known to lie. It could have been any one of them. The Enforcer kept the others in line. He was capable of killing infiltrators or waverers.'

'So, did he kill anyone?'

Ben cursed under his breath as the guard chose that moment to return with a tray of tea. After the soldier had departed, he repeated the question. 'He killed someone? Someone in the group?'

'I think you can infer the answer from my previous comment.'

Ben sighed. He remembered Henry's friend who had infiltrated this cabal and had been found dead – supposedly from auto-erotic asphyxia. But, as a life-long teetotaller, the amount of alcohol in his blood had told a different story. Ben knew that the truth about his death would never be publicised and his reputation would always remain tarnished. Ben inhaled deeply. Another reason to find the Enforcer.

He put his hands flat on the table. 'See, the Enforcer is a conundrum, as is the army officer. In the video, we could see from his shoulder to his groin. The others can all be identified – but not him.'

Knatchbull interrupted. 'The leader too. Why haven't you asked more about the leader?'

It was at this point that Ben knew he would have to use guile. He hadn't asked because he knew the leader to have been Stanley Murdock – but Knatchbull didn't know that he knew. He switched away from his main line of questioning. 'I haven't asked because last time you said you wouldn't tell me. Changed your mind?'

'No. That would give far too much away.'

'So no cake, just crumbs then.' As Ben said this, he felt his fingers start to itch. He had no idea why.

'Drink up your tea. It's getting cold. I persuaded them that I had to have best Darjeeling and Fortnum's biscuits. Compared to the cost of the personnel here to guard me, it's peanuts. Now, let's see, a single crumb for you? Not sure. What can I give you?'

Ben took out the four photos that had been retrieved from Murdock's box and placed them one at a time, face up, on the table. 'Know any of these?'

Knatchbull beamed. 'Oh, you are cleverer than I thought. I can see I'll have to be careful. I wonder where you got these.'

'What can you tell me about them?'

'As of last spring, two are alive and two are dead.'

'Care to tell me which?'

'No.'

'So what else can you tell me?'

There was a short silence. Ben opened his mouth to speak but Knatchbull waved him to silence. 'It has to be enough to whet their appetites but I must keep them guessing. Ah, yes. Here's a riddle for you. I got it from our leader and I'm not going to tell you if I've cracked it. See what you can do. Got a pen and paper?'

Ben produced a pen and a scrap of paper. 'This big enough?'

'It'll do.'

Knatchbull wrote, *B.H.S. She owns it all, Tavela, Arcadia.*

He passed the note across to Ben. Knatchbull rolled the pen between his thumb and fore-finger, then carefully placed it in his inside pocket.

'We're done for today, I think.'

'Is that it?'

'Come back when you need some more. Make it soon. I'm writing my memoir but it gets somewhat boring – can't put in the interesting bits, not in here anyway, nothing's sacred or secret here. Come back soon. I might help you with the riddle next time.' Knatchbull stood. 'I think I've said all I want to for the time being. But, can I ask a favour? They won't let me have internet. I get the FT and the Times – but they redact chunks by use of scissors. Could you get them to ease up on the scissors?'

'I'll try. In return, tell me how many lies you've told me this morning.'

Knatchbull put his head on one side. After a pause, he said, 'Just the one, I think.' And, with that, he turned and walked to the door. Ben was reminded of Henry's rude description of Knatchbull's posture. His bearing was certainly upright. Ben said, 'Grenadier Guards, wasn't it? That where you met that army officer?'

Knatchbull turned. 'I might tell you next time.' Then he knocked on the door to be let out.

Chapter 4

Katy unwrapped her gift from Mary – a kettle and four mugs.

'You'll need a kettle. Here's what you do. As soon as you've unpacked, go and knock on your neighbours' doors and ask them in for a cup of tea. They'll all be homesick or lost or just needing someone friendly to talk to. I did that and I made friends for life.'

Katy gave Mary a hug. 'I'm going to miss you all so much!'

Ben laughed. 'You are only going to be ten minutes walk away – but I bet we'll only see you when you've got washing to be done. If the washing machines are still in the bowels of the underground labyrinth there, I bet you'll be dropping off washing here and expecting someone to do it for you. Well, we won't.'

Mary added, 'Don't listen to him. We probably will. If you really need us to. Only a few days till you start. What are you going to do to fill your time?'

Katy looked embarrassed which amused her father. 'I've invited Chris round to help me solve that clue. He's on light duties so I thought he might be interested.'

Ben smiled at his daughter, 'You be kind to him.'

'Of course I will. He saved your lives, for God's sake. Why wouldn't I? And he's changed. The old Chris was hideous – hated him.' She blushed, which amused her father even more. He decided to change the subject.

'Have you got anywhere with the clue? Found out where Agatha Christie fits in?'

'OK, well, no. And I can't make out the cake bit at all.'

Ben thought about his tinkling fingers when he'd been with Knatchbull. That has been at the mention of cake. 'Read it to me again.'

'*The cake gets demolished and then there were Neele and the Colonel.*'

Ben laughed. 'Can you see the lightbulb going off in my head? The cake. I know what the cake is and I'm not going to tell you until we have Henry with us.'

'Dad, you can't! You are sooo mean. Don't you need to share it straight away?'

'No, Katy. I have long lost the impetuosity of youth. I can deal happily with delayed gratification and so must you.'

Mary added, 'Well, it's good we're getting somewhere, now that we have a second riddle to solve.' She pointed to Ben. 'And I don't want you to have to go back to that awful man to get help. Serious assistance needed. Let's ask Henry to dinner and have a brainstorm. You free Katy?'

'Yes, please. Can Chris come too?'

'Of course.' Ben looked at his watch. 'But first I've got to see Jim Spire. He says he'll be finishing the post mortem about now and I'm to pick up the body of Sir James Hutchinson. I'll see what news he has for me.'

'Oooh – I hope he was murdered. Henry thinks he was and Henry's awesome. D'you know, he has informants all across the old Soviet states. He's worried. He says we're all asleep because we're all in Russian pockets. He told me all about the break-up of Yugoslavia. What a mess, that was.'

If she was about to elaborate, she didn't as, at that moment, the doorbell rang and she ran to answer it.

* * *

'A bit old and shrivelled, a trifle frail but he could've lasted a few more years, I think.'

'So, he was murdered?'

Ben looked at Jim and Jim looked at the stooped man standing beside him. 'By the way, this is Peter Shepherd. He's from the Home Office.' Jim smiled. 'He's been looking over my shoulder to keep me in order.'

'Ben, good to meet you. You're a bit of a star in our neck of the woods.' And this told Ben that the Home Office might not be Peter Shepherd's normal place of abode. His department would definitely be more secret than that and would, in all probability, begin with an M.

'So, was he murdered?'

Jim pulled the sheet up over the body of Sir James Hutchinson and waved a finger at Ben. 'Well, Ben Burton. You're a dark horse. I've known you for God knows how long and you never told me about your more nefarious doings. A simple undertaker, I thought. But one who comes up with more than his fair share of murder victims. Peter tells me you're doing some work for the Home Office and then he got tight-lipped. Wouldn't say more. So that got me thinking, and the more I thought, the more I became convinced that "Home Office" is a euphemism. But for what?' He waved his hand in the air. 'No. Don't tell me. I'm happier just surmising.' He shook his head, then continued, 'And then I thought some more, and I the more I thought, the more I became convinced that it all started with Murdock. The story was that he was just a rich businessman who was kidnapped, well, that was a load of old hogwash, wasn't it?'

Peter Shepherd intervened. 'Jim, I don't think you want to go there.'

'Oh, but I do. I want to know what's going on.'

Ben raised a hand to Shepherd. 'We can trust Jim to be discreet.'

Shepherd shrugged. 'Your call.'

Ben decided on the shortened version. 'Stanley Murdock was involved in blackmail. So was Professor Dobson. They were also into other murky stuff, intelligence stuff, stuff that led to them being murdered.' He pointed to the covered corpse. 'As was this man here. The things they were involved in are covered by official secrets, hence Peter here being involved. The only innocent to have been killed was that poor nun, Sister Theresa. She got in the way of the person Murdock and Dobson were blackmailing. He was a local GP, a paedophile who'd known Murdock in Northern Ireland. Sister Teresa recognised him from way back so he killed her. So will you now answer my question. Was he murdered?'

'Thank you, Ben. Yes, of course he was.' Jim visible brightened. 'But this is the interesting part. He was killed in the same way as that poor nun. Injected with adrenaline. Her killer used a hypodermic but this poor man had at least three and probably more injections from epipens. Caused immediate cardiac dysrhythmia and subsequent cardiac arrest. He doesn't appear to have struggled. I'd say the epipens were administered very quickly.'

Ben's mind was turning fast. 'So probably more than one perpetrator?'

'That would fit.'

'Anything more you can tell me?'

'The lack of any struggle suggests he was attacked when he was resting, dozing, asleep maybe.'

Ben leaned in closer to Jim. 'I'm now going to tell you something I shouldn't. There was another case, possibly linked to this one. That one choked on a boiled sweet. Anything like that here?'

'No. If you're looking for similarities in methodology, from what you've just told me, I can't see any. This one had nothing in his oesophagus or trachea. If I can have a look at that other body, I'll see if I can find anything.'

'No joy there, I'm afraid. He's been cremated. Apparently, he was always sucking boiled sweets, so there were no suspicious circumstances until this man also died.'

'Pity that. I could have looked to see if he had the same tattoo. Old – been there some time. Care to see it?'

They moved over towards the body and Jim uncovered the feet of the corpse. 'It's on his right foot.' He pointed to a small tattoo near the base of the big toe.

Ben had trouble making it out. It looked like an oval red birthmark. 'What is it?'

Jim handed him a magnifying glass. He looked again. 'I can see now. It's a hand, a red hand.'

Jim said, 'UVF – protestant paramilitaries – people not to be crossed. Note that it's on his right foot. That's saying "No left footers here". I think your man might have been a victim of the Troubles, but fifteen years after they were supposed to have finished. So it's not just about blackmailers. Official secrets eh? IRA, INLA, New IRA. Be very careful, Ben. They're still operational and still dangerous.'

It was then that Ben remembered that Jim Spire had grown up in Ireland.

Chapter 5

Chris patted his stomach. 'Know what? I'm so glad I saved you two. Best meal I've had in weeks. Since my mum went home it's been takeaways and anything pre-cooked. S'pose, while I'm on light duties, I should learn to cook.'

Henry raised his glass to Chris. 'Good thought. Need to be able to look after yourself when you're back out in the field. Any idea when they're letting you back to leaping in front of bullets and the like?'

'Not for a while but I'm keeping them busy with my plans for the new homeless shelter at Downham. And Long John's not letting me goldbrick.'

Ben smiled. 'I suppose you mean shirk, slack, evade responsibility?'

'Yeah, s'going well. There's that big house for communal activities and a series of pods so they all have their own front door and privacy. Then, those snorers can do it all on their own and a good night's sleep can be had by the likes of me. It will be a thousand per cent better than the shelter where I met Long John and his mates – and I'm not exaggerating.'

Ben laughed then pointed towards Chris. 'That reminds me. I've been thinking we should take Long John to see Harris and the army high-ups – the ones organising the rehabilitation of Murdock's and Knatchbull's illicit army. He could be useful in giving them the low-down on what it's like to be abandoned by the army and thrown out on the streets. What d'you think?'

'Yeah. He'd love it. Wants to make up for lost time and he adores being a prima donna.'

'This is sooo interesting but do you think we could get onto the clues? I'm itching to see what Dad's come up with.' Katy reached into her pocket and brought out a copy of the sentence from Murdock's letter.

'Remind us, Katy.'

She read, *'The cake gets demolished and then there were*

Neele and the Colonel.' She put the paper on the table so they could all see it. 'The Colonel was Agatha Christie's husband and Nancy Neele was his lover. Caused some problems, I can tell you. She went doolally and disappeared. When they found her, she said she'd lost her memory. Agatha, that is. They bogged off and got married – Nancy and the faithless husband. I'd have got my revenge in, good and gory, but I don't think she ever did.'

Mary asked, 'Have you got further with the bad grammar?'

'Duh! Have you seen how many books she wrote? Bloody millions. I've got a list starting with Poirot. I'm trawling and Chris is helping. But, heh, good plots. How come she could think of so many? Clever woman. Now, enough about Agatha, what about the cake?'

Ben was not going to make it easy for his family. He thought he'd got it right, but examining his theory with these clever people would test its viability. 'Types of cake?'

Katy counted on her fingers as she listed them. 'Chocolate, lemon drizzle, carrot, red velvet, cheesecake, coffee and walnut. That's all I know. Your lemon drizzle's my favourite.'

'Go more traditional. Old fashioned cakes.'

Katy said, 'Mary, Henry, this is more you than me.'

Mary wrinkled her brow. 'Victoria sponge, madiera, fruit, caraway?'

Bens shook his head so Mary added, 'Another clue please.'

'German.'

'A German cake? Black forest gateau, stollen, bee sting cake?'

Chris looked horrified. 'With real bee stings?'

'No. I think it's called that because it's covered with honey but I've never made it. Sounds sickly sweet.'

Henry had been silent, then he roared with laughter. 'Murdock was such a devious sod, wasn't he? Got it. Of course. It's battenburg.'

Katy looked sideways at Henry. 'Explain please, to those of us who have never even heard of battenburg.' As she was talking, her fingers were moving fast on her phone. She held up a picture. 'Is the clue in the checky pattern?'

Henry replied, 'Nothing to do with the cake. It's in the

name.'

'Of course,' said Mary. 'They changed their name from Battenberg.'

Ben joined in. 'But I can't believe this could have been alluding to Louis. That was thirty years ago. The retaliation wouldn't have been delayed for so long.'

Katy banged her fist on the table. 'Can you please tell me what on earth you are talking about?'

Henry beamed at her. 'Sometimes, Katy, it's good to be old and wise and to have a long memory. The Battenbergs anglicised their name to Mountbatten when we went to war with Germany in 1914.'

Ben took up the tale. 'Louis Mountbatten was killed by the IRA in '79. It was that assassination that radicalised Jeremiah Knatchbull. Knatchbull was only a teenager but he idolised Louis. Louis was some sort of cousin and, more importantly, his mentor. Knatchbull is related to the Mountbattens.'

'I get it!' said Katy. 'This is what happened. The world has been informed that a member of the Mountbatten family is dead – Knatchbull – the cake demolished. But why would that lead to killing one, maybe two of the conspirators?'

Henry looked glum. 'If we can find out why, we'll be on the way to finding out who.'

'More worrying,' said Ben. 'How did they know who to target? Jim Spire mentioned the IRA, INLA and New IRA. We all thought this was sorted with Murdock and Knatchbull out of the way. If the Catholic paras have got wind of it, we're in big trouble.'

Chapter 6

'I know you want to get married soon but, at the moment, I just can't marry you.'

Mary had tried to explain it to Ben but Ben hadn't taken it in. He knew that she loved him and he was certain that he loved her. They were happy but he wanted to get married and to tell the world that he had moved on; that he had, at last, laid Diane's ghost to rest. 'Tell me again. Words of one syllable. What couldn't you find?'

'I went on-line. I had the date, the names, the place, but nothing. I could find no record of my marriage. I've got a paper certificate so I was going to take that to the register office where we were married. But it was twenty years ago and that office has closed. So I went to the Town Hall and asked what I should do. After a long sob-story, they arranged for me to go to see the archived entries. The storage facility is on a depressing industrial estate in East London and it's rammed to the rafters with old paperwork. Apparently, they can't dispose of it so, until it's digitised, they have to keep it somewhere. The man who met me knew more or less how it was organised. But still, it took us two hours to find the right ledger. Date and place were right but there was nothing in it corresponding to my paper certificate. I looked in the crease and I think a page has been removed but, if it was, it was done expertly, so I can't be sure.'

'Who would do that? And why?'

'I've a good idea who and why. My husband was Russian and he was a diplomat. He was killed here because MI6 was trying to recruit him, then his body was whisked back to Russia. MI6 would want to expunge all references to alliances between Sergei and Britain. But Sergei and I, we were so careful. I don't know how MI6 found out about us. And nothing was ever said to me or even hinted at. It's a complete mystery. But, until we've solved the mystery, I'm still married so we're in limbo.'

'What about Sergei's death certificate. Do you have that?'

'No. I looked through the records at the time of his death.

Remember, I was in the Services then so I had access. They must have taken his body back to Russia without a death certificate. I'm certain that no certificate was issued here.'

'Henry was around at that time. Maybe he can shed some light on it.'

* * *

'Sit down, my dear. I'm afraid I have some shocking news for you.'

Mary sat in the place indicated and replied, 'If it's shocking news, I'd better have a drink. I'd like one of your special g and t's please, Henry.'

'Jolly good idea. We'll all need one.' As he poured the drinks, Henry continued, 'Twenty years ago, Mary, you were told a big, fat, whopping lie. You were told that a Russian diplomat had been murdered in London and the Russians were dealing with it. You, my dear, were extremely clever so only a very few of us knew that you and Sergei were married. We have managed to protect you all these years but now you will have to know the truth.'

He handed each of them a large glass full to the brim. 'The Russians found out that we were trying to turn him. Sergei wasn't killed, but he was bundled back to Moscow. I was his contact and he managed to get just one message to me. He didn't know what his fate would be and, in order to protect you, he said I must destroy all evidence of your marriage and let you continue to believe he was dead. This I did.'

Mary sat in silence. She looked accusingly at Henry, then looked distraught. Ben took her hand and squeezed it gently. After a long pause, she said, 'Do we know what happened to him?'

'Ah, yes we do. He's alive, he's living in Southern Russia near the border with Ukraine and he's working for us.'

Mary gave him a look of pure fury. 'Henry! How could you? You left me in ignorance all these years. Why didn't you tell me? You let me mourn for him. I grieved for years. You saw what it did to me.'

'I know, my dear, and I'm sorry, truly sorry. Sergei didn't want you to know. He wanted you to get on with your life without him. He knew it would be safer for you. He also knew that he would never be allowed to come back to England. Then, as cover, he got married. He married a Ukrainian lady and they have a family.'

Mary sighed. 'My God, what a mess. He has children? How old are they?'

Henry nodded, 'The elder boy is getting on for sixteen, the girl a little older. Their youngest is five.'

'How old is the girl?'

'She's eighteen.'

'So she was born soon after he was taken back. Is he happy?'

'Let's say he's content. And he's sending me very useful intel.'

Ben remembered a conversation with Henry in Front Court the previous year. He spoke for the first time. 'So Sergei is your useful contact in Ukraine?'

'Yes. He owns a haulage firm and travels into Crimea regularly. He has a web of agents across the whole of Eastern Europe and sends me their news. As for not telling you, my dear, I couldn't. It was Sergei's secret not mine. In my defence, I lost contact with him for years. I didn't know if he was alive or dead. He found me again just five years ago. It was in 2008 when Georgia was invaded. Sergei had information he needed to share. I have asked him more than once if I could tell you about him. His reply has always been that I should tell you only if you asked. You have asked and I am truly sorry to have to drop this bombshell on you, but it was his decision not mine.'

Mary was silent for some time gazing into the distance. Ben and Henry waited in silence. Then she squeezed Ben's hand. She spoke in a low voice, as if to herself. 'Suddenly I know what it feels like to have your world turned upside-down; to have all you believed to be true blown away in a fine mist of deceit. It will take time to assimilate.' Then she turned to Ben. 'But I have you. And I don't have to carry any guilt. Plus, I have the bonus of knowing he's alive and has built a life for himself with which he is content. I can do the same.' She paused. 'But I will never be content.'

Ben's heart lurched. Whatever was coming, he would have to deal with it.

Mary smiled at him. 'I'm not content with contentment. I'm

going to be happy.'

Henry was the first to dab his eyes.

Then Mary sat up straight. 'Another g and t please Henry and tell us what Sergei has been sending you.'

'It's all too depressing. Millbank are listening but the politicians are being cloth-eared. They want to trade with Putin. They don't realise that, if you snuggle up to the Russian bear, it will have only one outcome. Let's leave it for another day.'

'OK. Yes. Today we celebrate the fact that there's no record of my previous marriage so we can get married. Henry, hurry up with those drinks.'

Ben was lost in two competing thoughts. He ruminated on his enormous good fortune at finding such a woman. This vied with a sudden increase in concern for the world order way beyond Northern Ireland.

Chapter 7

Tommy was visiting from Ireland so Ben was preparing a very special meal. Tommy had spent a week in Brighton with his children, Virginia and Alistair Murdock and Virginia's fiancé, Gavin, and now he was stopping off with Ben and Mary before travelling back to Moira. They hadn't seen him since their visit to Moira when they'd collected Murdock's videos from him; those same DVDs that had exposed a genocidal plot and had set a myriad of hares running. That recording and the discovery of Murdock's stash of paperwork had put Jeremiah Knatchbull in his very own personal gaol and had ensured that MI5 knew the identities of the other conspirators – all except one – that elusive soldier. Now, it seemed possible that these conspirators were being murdered.

Ben and Mary had invited Henry as Ben felt sure that he and Tommy would get on. Katy had also been invited and had asked if she could bring Chris, and that they might be late as they had 'something vital' that they had to do. Ben had suggested that she shouldn't be too late as she still had all her packing to do and she was supposed to be ensconced at Ethel's in two days.

Mary wandered into the kitchen. 'Smells good.'

'Well, I thought he'd have been fed by Gavin over the past few days so I had to put some effort in. I'm doing fish chowder like we had in Galway, followed by Suffolk pork in a cep sauce. Then I ran out of ideas so it's apple crumble and strawberry coulis.'

'Sounds delicious. Gavin's certainly become one of the family down in Brighton. And Virginia is so happy with him. Wouldn't it be wonderful if Alistair could find a soulmate. He's lovely and he'd make someone a wonderful husband. Talking of husbands, what are we going to do about this wedding. What do you think about having a big do?'

Ben sighed inwardly. This put him in a quandary. He would love to have a small wedding, one that Katy would term 'sedate'. He certainly didn't want a disco or, worse still, karaoke. 'What do you want?'

But Mary didn't seem to have heard. 'Ben, I know you want

to put a line under your past and allow Diane's ghost to rest in peace. A big wedding would do that. It would tell the world that you have moved on.'

Ben could feel his shoulders slump as he bowed to the inevitable but Mary hadn't finished. 'But I know you, and I think a small and intimate wedding followed by us visiting all of our more distant friends would suit you better. But it's for you to say. I'll go with whatever you want.'

Ben took her in his arms and kissed her. 'Mary, you are an angel sent from the Heaven that I don't believe in. A small wedding. Is that OK for you?'

She hugged him back. 'Perfect.' Then she grinned. 'And so much easier to organise. I'll start a list.'

* * *

'My, but it's grand to see you again. And no sneaking around in the middle of the night this time. It's a fine home you have here, Ben. And I hear congratulations are in order. Well now, I have some grand news too.' Tommy stepped into the kitchen and Mary opened her arms and enveloped him in a warm hug.

'It's wonderful to see you, Tommy. Now, would you like a nice cup of Irish tea?'

Tommy fished a bottle of champagne out of his bag. 'Put this in the fridge, will you. And a cup of good strong tea will keep me going till we can celebrate in style.'

Tommy was hopping from foot to foot. Ben thought he might be in need of the loo so responded by asking, 'Do you need to freshen up after your journey?'

Tommy beamed at them both. 'No, no. But I can't keep my news in any longer. I'm going to be a grandda. Ginny and Gavin are expecting and I'm going to be a grandda. All these years wondering where my children were and if they were all right. Then I find them, I have a family and next thing I know, my family's growing. Isn't that just grand.'

Mary hugged him again. 'Oh Tommy, I'm so pleased.'

Tommy was still grinning. 'I know. They survived being brought up by that Murdock and now my Ginny and Allie are bringing me purpose in my old age. But there's more. It's twins so I'll be a grandda twice over. A boy and a girl, they think. The only sad thing is that she's missing her mammy. But Allie's being like a mother hen and Gavin's delighted so she'll be well looked after.'

Mary was immediately in organising mode. 'That is so brilliant. I'll go and see her. See if she needs an older woman to talk to.'

Ben laughed. 'Mary, you're only ten years older than she is, but it's a fine thought. I'm sure they'll appreciate all our support.'

At this point the doorbell rang and Henry was ushered in. After the introductions, where Henry shook Tommy firmly by the hand for an inordinate amount of time, Henry waded in. 'Delighted, dear boy. Delighted to meet you at last and thank you in person. It's thanks to you that we've foiled those evil bastards – so far, anyway. But it seems that we may have a further problem. Has Ben told you about the new murder – two murders, I believe?'

Mary stepped in. 'Henry, the poor man has only just arrived.'

'Yes but we need to move fast – and this man knows how the IRA works so we need to pick his brains.'

'Henry, I haven't been involved with the Provos in more than fifteen years.'

Henry interrupted, 'Of course, of course. But the mindset of the diehards doesn't change. If they're picking off our ancient plotters, we'll need to get inside their heads.'

Tommy looked around. 'These walls don't have ears, do they?'

Ben shook his head. 'We've had GCHQ sweep them – just in case. MI5 paid for it and we have their assurance that we're clean.'

'Hope so. What I'm about to tell you needs to be passed on but with the proviso that it didn't come from me. I keep my ear to the ground, I still have friends who know things, but I value my life, especially now. Understand?'

Mary responded by squeezing his hand. 'One hundred per cent. So far, we've kept your identity a secret between us and we'll continue with that. MI5 knows nothing of you and we'll keep it that way. You deserve some happiness.' She sat up straight. 'And we'll make sure you get it.'

Ben looked at the clock. 'You'd better tell us what you want us to know before Katy gets here. She's bringing Chris and he's MI5. So, between the four of us, for now. Yes?'

They all nodded. Tommy continued, 'Well, it's like this. Since Cameron's announcement in January that there'd be an EU referendum, there have been stirrings. See, the Provos like it the way it is. They were promised that they'd eventually get a united Ireland if they gave up the armed struggle and, if the UK leaves the EU they see that prospect moving further away. And they don't like it. They're jittery – and they've the added problem of stopping the hot-heads in the New IRA from doing anything stupid.'

Henry asked, 'Do they know about the Murdock plot?'

'Jesus, that was a bad one. Kill all the Catholics. I haven't heard that anything's leaked but my sources aren't close to the centre. So I can't answer that one for sure.'

Ben had a flash of inspiration. Maybe the four photos from Murdock's box could help them. He removed them from his pocket and placed them on the table in front of Tommy. 'Are these IRA?'

Tommy's bark of a laugh seemed, at first, to be inappropriate. 'Ben, where, in the name of God, did you get these? No, don't answer that. I don't want to know.' He prodded the photos. 'You couldn't be more wrong about these fellas.' He divided the photos in two. He pointed to the ones on his left. 'These two, you've no need to worry about. Killed, must be two years since. Lured into a trap in Border Country. Their bodies won't be found.'

'And the other two?'

'Codenamed Bill and Ben. Catholic paras have been searching for them since the start of the Troubles.' He pointed again. 'These are hard men, hit men, Prods. The four of them, they were killers but they were protected.' He tapped the side of his nose. 'Unofficial protection from on high. I found that out from my stint in the RUC. Police get to know things. It's rumoured they learnt their dark arts years since and they're still operational. And they'll work for anyone who can pay them well. Just as long as it's Prods they're working for and the hits are Catholic.'

'Know their real names?'

'No. The only other thing I know is that they're Scots not Irish and that they came originally from Glasgow.'

Ben and Henry exchanged glances. Henry chuckled. 'So the Rangers v Celtic animosity has taken a rather more sinister turn. '

They were just about to start dinner when Katy and Chris arrived. There were hurried introductions where Tommy was introduced as a friend from Moira. When it was also revealed that he was Alistair and Virginia Murdock's father, his hand was seriously pumped by Chris, he was given a big hug by Katy and huge grins were exchanged all round.

They chatted about family events and Katy stood to propose a toast to 'Ginny and her lovely man.' They drank the toast then Katy added, 'I was wondering if maybe they'd want a godmother, even one who didn't believe in an afterlife but sure would love those babies.' Then she turned to Chris. 'You could be a godfather.'

At this, Chris nearly fell off his chair, shaking his head and muttering, 'No way.'

It was agreed that the next day, Henry would give Tommy a tour of Ethel's and Mary would take him round Cambridge while Ben and Katy finished preparing Sir James Hutchinson for viewing.

But first Ben had a phonecall to make. He congratulated Virginia on her expected new arrivals then asked the question that had been bugging him. 'Was Stanley Murdock an Agatha Christie fan?'

Her reply confirmed some of his suspicions and raised some questions. 'Oh no. It was Mother who was the real fan. Father always expressed disgust at what he called "the vacuity of her plots", but he could argue points in detail so he must have read all the books. Lucien would have a ding-dong with him sometimes – you know, that father-son alpha male thing. And sometimes Mother would disagree with him but it was usually a one-sided argument because we were all too scared to disagree for long. But that made him mad too because he wanted to prove the point that he knew more than Agatha Christie. There really was no pleasing him.'

Chapter 8

'I'm going to miss you. Especially as you haven't solved that Agatha clue yet. What have you and Chris been doing? And don't answer that!'

Ben and Katy had been working on Sir James Hutchinson's body. This would be the last time Katy would assist him before her departure to St Etheldreda's College.

'Yeah, but you've still got Michael and he's brought Pam in to help. I never thought she'd leave the force but she said it was a choice between her career and Michael – and she chose Michael. Good pick. The police are so up-their-own-arses. Just cos he's been to jail, she wouldn't progress. How's that for discrimination!'

'It's left Sarah with a problem. Now her best friend's gone…'

'And she hasn't come out at work. When she didn't get that promotion in Bristol, it really hurt. But Dani's solid so she'll be OK. Heh, she might come and join you here.'

Ben shuddered. He and Sarah were too much alike to work together in harmony. He broached the subject that had been on his mind for some weeks. 'I wanted to talk to you. I'm thinking of a sort of semi-retirement or doing something different altogether. I raised it with Michael and he wants to buy the business. What do you think?'

'Oh, Dad, yes. You and Mary could go off spying together. And Henry and I will cheer you on from the alternative universe at Ethel's. That should work.'

'Good, that's settled then.' Ben pointed to the body in front of them, 'But first, I've got to meet this man's co-conspirators. I'm seeing three of them this afternoon. They wanted to come and view. I'll go and see the rest after Tommy's gone back home.

* * *

Ben was glad that Katy was absent from the meeting with Lord

Thornhill and Messrs Ingleby and Asquith, the three conspirators who had decided to view the deceased. The attitude she'd expressed about the police would have been magnified with these three. They had arrived together, chatting amicably. They looked to be in their late sixties or early seventies, sprightly and healthy. The first thing Ben noticed was their loud voices. They reminded him of those over-confident and privileged young men who regularly tumbled out of their colleges in Cambridge and into the local hostelries. Ben took an instant dislike when Thornhill addressed him as he would a servant. He decided that swallowing his pride and acting with servility might get him the answers he needed. He arranged for teas and coffees to be brought, alerted Mary to stay within eavesdropping distance, then sat the three of them down in 'the relatives room'.

'I am most terribly sorry to have kept you; a weeping relative. Firstly, may I say how sorry I am for your loss. Can I ask how well you knew Sir James?'

Thornhill answered, 'Don't know what concern it is of yours, but we've known Jimmy for several years.'

Ben replied, 'It is a concern. If people are close, viewing the body of the deceased may affect them more than they had anticipated. I like to be prepared.'

Ben looked closely at the three men before him. Thornhill seemed to be the leader, and Ben quickly decided he would probably get nothing of value from him. Asquith was looking distracted so might be a useful source of information. Ingleby was cowering in the corner, having pushed his chair back as far as he could. Ben needed to separate them so, after a preliminary description of the process, he asked them in which order they would like to view their erstwhile friend.

Ingleby spoke for the first time. 'I thought we'd all be going in together.' He continued in little more than a whisper, 'I don't think I can face it alone.' Ben decided that Ingleby should go last.

'Good God man!' This was Thornhill. 'Don't be such a wimp. Of course you can go in alone. I'll go first.'

* * *

As he'd surmised, Ben had got little from Thornhill. Lord Thornhill had looked on his former co-conspirator and his only remark had been, 'Saw him a couple of weeks ago. He looks better now than he did then.'

When Ben had enquired about their last meeting, Thornhill had added, 'Went to tell him about poor old Braybrooke. Silly bugger choked on one of those confounded sweets he was always eating. Jimmy was too frail to go to the funeral. Good do. Doubt you'll be able to match it.'

Asquith had come next. When asked how he'd known the deceased, he'd been open about the fact that they'd been in a group of 'like-minded individuals' but it had been disbanded 'many years ago'. When Ben had asked if he'd also known Braybrooke, Asquith had been visibly shaken, until Ben had added that Thornhill had mentioned him. Then he'd replied with the rider, 'I knew him, but not well.'

When Thornhill and Asquith had asked directions to the nearest hostelry and had told Ingleby they'd meet him there, Ben had been delighted that he would be able to get Ingleby alone. He waited until they were out of earshot.

'Mr Ingleby, you seem to be most distressed by the death of your friend. Is there any way I can help? You know that you don't have to view his body if it will upset you further.'

'Oh, I must. I must.' Ingleby drew himself up and breathed in deeply. 'Thank you. You are very kind but I promised him, you see.'

'You promised him?'

'Yes. It's been a terrible shock – his death. I saw him only two weeks ago and I promised him. He was worried that he might die and he wanted a good send off. I'm sure you'll do him proud.'

'I understand, and we will do our very best for him. But, I gather he was rather frail and I'm afraid death comes to us all. Was he ill?'

'Oh no. He thought he might be murdered.'

Ben replied with much surprise in his voice, 'Murdered? Whatever made him think that?'

'Braybrooke. We all knew Braybrooke, and his death unsettled Jimmy. It's unsettled me too. Jonathan had been to see him and put the fear of God into him. He wouldn't say more. Anyway, said too much.'

'Jonathan?'

'Jonathan Sandys. He was one of our group. But, as I say, I've said too much. I need to see that Jimmy is looking serene. If he'd been murdered, I'm sure I'd be able to tell. So I've got to see him.'

'I'm sure we can put your mind at rest. He does look serene and did so when he arrived. Do you know why he feared that he might be murdered?'

'It was something bad in our past. He said he was going to atone for it. Going to tell the truth. And then he died.' Ingleby shuddered. 'So, Mr Burton, I think we're all doomed to die in silence.'

'Did he tell you who he thought might be out to kill him?'

'That's the terrible thing. He thought it was one of ours not one of theirs.' Ingleby looked stricken. 'Forget I said that. Maudlin nonsense. Take no heed.'

'Have you told anyone of your fears?'

'I haven't told the others. They already think I'm a wimp. If I told them, they'd think I'm paranoid. What do you think? Do you think Jimmy was murdered?'

Ben decided not to answer that one directly. Instead he said, 'Shall we go in and see him. Then you can see that he looks at peace.'

Chapter 9

It was Tommy's last night with them. As soon as they'd finished eating, Katy took the stage. Ben had already warned her that Tommy, a lovely man and the biological father of Virginia and Alistair Murdock, still had friends in the IRA. She showed the clue to Tommy and read it aloud to him, *'The cake gets demolished and then there were Neele and the Colonel.'* She explained, 'It's from Stanley Murdock and we know that Murdock was real keen on correct usage. That got us started. And we know that the front end refers to Knatchbull, another conspirator who everyone thinks is dead. So that's the cake getting demolished. We were getting nowhere with the back end although we know it was Agatha Christie. She's written shedloads of stuff which we were wading through and then Chris got this brainwave. He wrote a letter to the Cambridge News saying he was researching Agatha and could anyone help. And someone could, so we went to see her today.'

Katy stopped and took a slow sip of her wine. The silence lengthened. Ben laughed. 'OK drama queen, tell us what happened next.'

'Well, she was a mine of info. She's a famous author and she's been a Christie fan forevs. She's talking to the Agatha people and they're going to let her write more Poirot books so she must know her stuff. You want to know what she told us?'

Henry replied, 'My dear girl, you know you've got us all on tenterhooks. I'm a very old man and I could pop my clogs at any time. So could you please put us out of our misery and give us the punchline.'

'OK. So we told her to ignore the cake bit and it was *"and then there were"* that got her going. Apparently, Agatha wrote this book yonks ago – like seventy years. It had a naughty title that we wouldn't use today. So they changed the name to Ten Little Indians. Then they must have decided that that was a bit naff too. Now it's called And Then There Were None. We would have been here earlier but we had to go and buy the book.'

Chris held up two copies. 'We got one each cos we knew

we'd argue over it.' He grinned at Katy and she poked out her tongue in return.

To Ben, that looked like chemistry. He knew how far he'd come on his path from hypervigilance when he realised he could view this liaison with equanimity despite the difference in their ages – and the fact that Chris was a spy. He smiled broadly. Mary smiled back and gave him a thumbs-up. He wondered briefly whether Mary might be a witch, as she seemed to be able to read his mind.

'So our job now is to read the book. Well, Chris has to cos I've got to move my stuff to Ethel's so I'll be busy. I'll do the Wiki version.'

Mary asked, 'Can I have your copy then?'

'Brill – yes please. Then I can just do Wiki with a clear conscience.'

Chapter 10

On an encrypted phonecall, Ben alerted Parker to the provenance of the two extant photo villains. MI5 would be following up in Glasgow. He asked if Parker had discovered any more about the army Torso-man and Parker responded in the negative. There were no distinguishing features to the uniform, the portion on view in the video being devoid of any adornments.

Parker told Ben that MI5 had separately warned each of the conspirators that there were rumours of a plot, and each had been asked if they had been involved. Dire warnings had been given, no matter what their response had been. To Parker's obvious delight, one of the conspirators, Geoffrey Asquith, had turned 'queen's evidence' as soon as questioned. He'd wanted to 'come clean at last'. The crux of his evidence had been that there were some 'true believers' among the group but some had been drawn in and then they'd been frightened to leave as they were terrified of Murdock. Although Murdock had threatened them with 'an Enforcer', they had never known the identity of this person. Asquith had told Parker that those who had been brave enough to share their thoughts, had decided that the Enforcer had to be the army officer who was present at just one of the meetings, the one on the video, but had not been introduced. Murdock had also made sure of their compliance by describing what the IRA would do to them if they were ever unfortunate enough to be delivered into their hands. And he had intimated that he would not be averse to being the deliverer.

Ben then told Parker that he wanted to see Asquith again before Hutchinson's funeral and groaned when told that Asquith lived in Devon. Devon was a long drive from Cambridge. He brightened a bit on learning that another conspirator, Jonathan Sandys, also lived down there, two birds etc. He brightened further when Mary agreed to join him on the trip. They arranged to meet both Asquith and Sandys the following day, ostensibly to talk about Hutchinson's impending funeral. Ben had finished the phonecall by suggesting that Parker might like to read some Agatha Christie. Ben wondered what Parker would make of that.

* * *

Sandys was the first to be interviewed as he lived near Brixham, further than Asquith's Tiverton. Ben's rationale for this was twofold. Asquith would assuredly be the better informant so seeing Sandys first might give them further questions to ask of Asquith. The other, less weighty reason, was that starting the journey home from Tiverton might make it seem shorter.

They were met at the door of a pristine bungalow on the edge of Brixham by an upright man probably in his late sixties. He shook them both by the hand with a firm grip, bowing slightly over Mary's hand. He introduced himself. 'Jonathan Sandys.' He pronounced it Sands. 'Come in. I really don't know why you have come all this way. I'm sure I could have sent you an email.' Sandys waited. This had obviously been a question.

Ben answered, 'Thank you so much for seeing us. We must confess to mixing business with pleasure. We've not been to this part of the world for years and rather fancied the trip. Your friend, Sir James Hutchinson, is already prepared and awaiting his funeral so we had a couple of days spare. I hope it isn't an inconvenience but there were a few names underlined in his address book so we assumed these were important to him. Yours was one of those.'

'Was it indeed? Now, that's interesting.'

As there had been no underlinings, nor indeed any address book in his possession, Ben shrugged. 'As you know, he was the last of his family so we have taken on the duty of making his funeral meaningful to those who attend. At the moment, that could be far from the case. His public life, we know about. We have contacted everyone in the book but still know very little of his personal life. We haven't received much response from those underlined. So we are hoping that, by visiting, we can persuade you to give us some background information to make his send-off appropriate. Any insights you can give us would be much appreciated.'

Sandys took a while to answer. He closed his eyes and stroked his chin. It was Ben's belief that this pause was to give him time to decide what, if anything, it was safe to divulge. Sandys answered with a question. 'Who else was underlined?'

Ben had been prepared for this. Mary delved into her briefcase and produced a list – it was the list of conspirators.

Andrews
Asquith
Braybrook
Hutchinson
Ingleby
Overton
Sandys
Sheringham
Thornhill

She handed it to Sandys. Ben watched his face as he scanned the list. For a split second, Sandys' face showed alarm. He recoiled in his seat and the list trembled in his hand. Then he waved it away. 'I know these people. Good men all. But I haven't seen any of them in years.'

Ben knew this to be a lie on two counts. Sandys had been to Braybrook's cremation and Asquith had told Parker that, after Braybrook's death, Jonathan Sandys had visited Sir James Hutchinson and had 'put the fear of God into him'. Could Sandys be the Enforcer? Ben was watching closely but, after his initial reaction, Sandys' stiff upper lip had resolutely refused to quiver. He was certainly a cool customer. They spent a further hour with Sandys but got no more useful information. They were not asked, and didn't volunteer, that they were also visiting Sandys' co-conspirator Geoffrey Asquith.

* * *

Geoffrey Asquith welcomed them into his spacious home and seated them with ready-prepared coffee and little biscuits. Of course, he had no idea that they were anything but undertakers so they had to be careful not to reveal what they had learnt from Parker. On their way there, they had decided what they could divulge from their conversation with Sandys and what they could concoct as having been said by Sandys. And they'd decided that Mary was to lead this time.

Unlike Sandys' house in Brixham, this one had no view of the sea, but, to Ben's mind, its proximity to the M5 was a godsend.

Ben opened the conversation by thanking Asquith for having invited them into his home. Ben was on high alert for both verbal and non-verbal clues and he knew Mary would be doing likewise. As an aside, he wondered why Mary was so much better at picking up those small clues than he was.

Mary smiled at Asquith, with what Ben called 'her winning smile'. 'We were coming to see Mr Sandys anyway and were a little concerned about your agitated state when we saw you, so we thought we'd have to look in to see if you were OK.'

'Thank you. That's so very kind of you. Yes, I was a bit unsettled, but I've got some things off my chest – things that were bothering me – so I feel much better now.'

Mary beamed. 'I thought you were looking a little calmer. We're delighted, aren't we, Ben?' Ben nodded his delight as Mary continued, 'Mr Sandys was a little concerned about you.'

Asquith's hand shook as he put down his cup. As he leaned forward, his face was hidden. He placed the cup and saucer on the low table and held onto the saucer for longer than he needed to. When he looked up, his expression was defiant. 'Don't mention that man to me. He threatened poor old Jimmy. Said he'd kill him if he told. That's why I thought he'd been murdered. But now Ingleby's told me Jimmy died in peace, I can rest easy.' He paused and they waited. After a few seconds he continued, 'Anyway, Sandys probably hasn't got it in him. He's like all bullies, all talk.' He paused again, and again they waited in silence. 'It was so soon after Braybrook, you see. Sorry, said too much again. You mustn't mind me. When you get old, you get silly ideas.'

'Don't worry,' said Mary. 'We meet a lot of people in distress and we know that sometimes their feelings get the better of them. We understand.'

'You're very kind. Yes, this has brought back memories. Memories that I'd rather forget. I'll have to see Sandys at the funeral, but then, I never want to see any of them again.'

'But Mr Sandys seemed so affable. He gave us some useful background on Sir James.'

'Don't be taken in by his manner. He's an evil man. Now, there, I've said it. Evil, through and through.'

Chapter 11

The day was fine, the burial service and interment had gone without a hitch. Ben had been surprised by the paucity of 'followers'. Despite the obituary in The Times, only thirty guests had attended. All were now ensconced, at MI5's expense, in a room at Trinity, Sir James's old college. That morning, the building had been swept for bugs and explosives and everyone entering or leaving had been asked for ID. The excuse had been that some 'very important people' were to be in attendance later.

The remaining seven named conspirators were all present. The other attendees would undoubtedly be secretly filmed and identified. Ben recognised one serving MP – a member of the Government, he thought. He was probably the excuse for the increased security. A cohort of MI5 officers, whose expertise at balancing trays of food and drink was variable, were circulating discreetly and no doubt listening intently to the conversations. The gaggle of conspirators had gathered in one corner of the room, a room rather too ornately decorated for Ben's taste. This group was being plied with copious quantities of food and drink – so much so, that another mourner called one of the 'waiters' over to suggest that their group was being short-changed. This oversight was immediately rectified.

Ben surveyed the other guests. If the army officer from the conspiracy video was present, he was being ignored by the other members of the 'annihilate the Catholics' conspiracy. None of the other guests had a military bearing so Ben assumed he was absent. He would have to ask Parker. As Ben was watching proceedings, he saw Asquith quietly remove himself from his group and walk swiftly over to talk to Mary. He then hurried out of the building. Ben followed and saw him getting into a taxi. 'The station please. And quickly.' And he was gone.

As Ben returned, Mary approached him. 'He said we'd be busy; that another one of them was going to die.'

* * *

When they got home, the answerphone was flashing. There was a message from Tommy to phone him urgently. Ben immediately dialled Tommy's number and put it on speakerphone so Mary could listen too. The phone was answered on the first ring. 'Ah, grand. Ben, now listen. I have a sma'tle bit of news for ye. Them fellas we was discussing, they're all in a tiswas about this referendum thing about the EU. I got a whiff that something's afoot your side of the water. They're mobilising, looking for trouble, that's for sure. As far as I can tell, they've not got wind of that thing I gave you but there's murmurings all over. You've got to keep a lid on it. Or, if the lid's already off, get it back on, quick as you like.'

'Have you heard anything specific?'

'I'm not near enough to get the details – all I know is they're on alert. And that should put your people on alert too.'

'Thanks Tommy. I'll pass the message on.'

'That's all I wanted to say. Be very careful, you two. My children are fond of you so you'd better stay safe.' And with that he rang off.

'Well,' said Mary. 'That raised more questions than it answered. The natives are restless but we have no idea what they're going to do. Nor do we know if they are behind our murder. Or indeed, if it was one or two murders. And does he really think we're in danger because I can't see how we can be.'

'No. I can't see how the IRA or its off-shoots would know anything about us. It was the Protestant militia not the Catholics who ran us out of Moira. Anyway, we can forget about them for a while. I've made arrangements with Chris that we'll go to see Long John. I hear that Chris's new homeless shelter in Norfolk is coming on apace. D'you know, every time I think of it, I get a warm glow. And your idea of funding it from the money Dobson left me was a brainwave. Dobson did so much damage in his life, then he redeemed himself just before he was murdered. It's good that he's making further recompense in his afterlife.'

* * *

They hadn't heard from Henry for two days so decided that, before their trip to Norfolk, they would go to see him to check on him and give him an update. When they arrived at his door in Ethel's, they could hear hoots of laughter – Henry's low growl and a higher, lighter chuckle. They knocked and waited and Ben found himself unsurprised to have the door opened by his daughter.

'Hi Dad. Hi Mary. Come in. Henry was just scandalising me with tales of his nefarious exploits.'

'Ah, Ben. Come in, come in. And Mary, my favourite amour.' He turned to Katy, 'She refused to marry me, you know.'

Katy laughed again. 'But you asked me to marry you too – remember? Then you rescinded the offer before I could answer. You said you were too old for me.'

'Oh yes. See, I really am getting old – I'd forgotten that. Too old and too gay.'

'And too busy to keep in touch,' added Ben.

'Fraid so. I've been deep in matters Russian. He's got territorial ambitions and we're ignoring all the signs.' He shook his head. 'Enough of my maudlin nonsense. Your brilliant daughter here has had to do some serious work. Nose to the grindstone stuff. So, I'm afraid we've rather neglected you.'

'Yeah, Dad. It's real hard. There's stuff I've never seen before. But there's a couple of public school boys who've been really helpful. So what's happening with your group of oldies? Still getting murdered?'

Ben answered. 'Thankfully, just the one that we know of and the other suspected. We have one turned queen's evidence who says it's an inside job and he thinks there will be more. We have nothing to connect the IRA to it – but that doesn't mean they aren't in it up to their necks. It seems some of the conspiracy group were true believers and some just scared stiff of Murdock and his Enforcer. And we don't yet know who the Enforcer was. We've found out that Sandys is a bully. Could be any of them – except Asquith. He's the one dishing the dirt.'

'So no progress, then. Got anywhere with the clues?'

Mary answered. 'Getting nowhere fast. I'm reading that Agatha book, "And Then There Were None". It's really good. But I'm not sure where that takes us. All we've surmised so far is that this whole shabang was set off by the news that Knatchbull is dead – even though we know he isn't.'

Ben joined in. 'And we have no idea about the other clue, the one from Knatchbull. They were all owned by Philip and Tina Green but we can't get any further.'

Henry said, 'Remind us of the quote.'

Mary brought her notebook from her bag and showed them the second clue – the one Ben had got when he'd visited Knatchbull in his solitary state in his secret gaol. *B.H.S. She owns it all, Tavela, Arcadia.*

'We've researched Philip and Tina Green till we're sick to death of them and we can't see how they're connected to all this. I've even asked Parker and he's been digging where I can't go. Nothing. I don't want to but I think I'll have to go and see Knatchbull again. He said he'd get us started if we couldn't do it alone.'

'Dad! You can't give in. Listen, I've got a tutorial tomorrow morning then I'll have a bit of time to look at it. Can you leave it till then?' She looked again at the quote and photographed it with her phone. She pointed to each word as she counted them. Then she added, 'And can I have a list of the conspirators including the two dead ones. I've got the beginnings of an idea.'

'Can do. We're off to meet up with Chris and Long John in Norfolk to see how the shelter's coming on. Haven't seen Long John since he brought Chris back to life with his singing.' Ben looked across and could see three pairs of shiny eyes.

Katy mopped hers and blew her nose. 'Whoever would have thought that Ilkley Moor would bring someone out of a coma. Give him a big hug from me.'

Ben smiled. 'D'you mean Chris or Long John?'

They all saw Katy turn away to hide her blushes but they made no comment.

Chapter 12

Ben could swear that Long John was looking ten years younger than the last time they'd met. He had a spring about him that had been missing before, and Ben could hear that John's breathing was no longer as laboured as it had been. Such were the benefits of living in a warm and dry environment, Ben suspected. That and not being turfed out to roam the streets all day. They'd exchanged manly hugs and a few back-slaps and Long John had taken them to show them his 'pod'. It was one of a line of five – all sparkling new and all self-contained. It was about the size of a shipping container with all mod cons. The pods stood in the gardens of a large house. The house was barely visible, such was the scaffolding and plastic sheeting in which it was encased.

'Col's this way. Talking to people. Summat to do with the build.'

Ben was reminded that Chris had called himself Col when he'd been living in homeless shelters while hiding from Knatchbull. Obviously his friends from the shelters still thought of him as 'Col'.

Mary was the one to state the obvious. 'It's amazing! Sell one medium sized house in a posh part of Cambridge and you can buy all this? How big is the house?'

'Aye lass. It don't make sense te me neither. There'll be twelve bedrooms in t'house and twenty pods in t'first place. Then Col says you're selling another house for t'next stage. Then army says they'll fund costs for ex-army te get em on their feet, like. I'll be helping in that seeing as how I've been like that meself. Col's setting up the charity – all way beyond me. He's talking to some people called emus and getting advice from them.'

Ben decided he'd better talk to Chris about the emus.

* * *

When Chris had stopped laughing, he said, 'Trust John! It's Emmaus not emus. They've been amazing – and John Harris has been doing his bit from the army side. I think he's feeling guilty that they couldn't stop me being shot at your meet with Knatchbull.' He grinned. 'I'm milking that. And I'm taking Long John to meet some army bigwigs – organised by Harris. He thinks he can persuade more money out of them if they see a real ex-squaddie making good. We're working on the medical side too – getting some psychos on board.'

'Psychos?'

'Sorry. Technical term. Psychologists, psychiatrists. Alison Clare and the Friary are helping there.' Chris touched the side of his nose. 'Not what you know but who you know, eh.'

'So it's turning into a big operation?'

'Yeah. We want it to be the best place in Britain for rehabilitating ex-soldiers. And that's where my Service comes in. We're starting with the list of Murdock's conscripts to his army of malcontents. Two birds – stop them being recruited to undercover armies and give them something worthwhile to live for instead. Dr Clare says it'll be a long job with some of them.'

Mary gave Chris a quick hug. 'This life really suits you. You look happier than I've ever seen you.'

'Yeah, I am. It's all thanks to my "road to Damascus" moment. Mine came on the A10, remember? Road to Downham – when John and his mates offered me half their earnings; £1.34 if I remember rightly. Now, they're all busy here earning a wage and it's a damn sight more than £1.34. They're used to a life in the open so they're in charge of the garden. It's huge and it's a jungle so they've got their jobs cut out. They need me to tell them what to do but I'm training them up to be self-sufficient and make their own decisions.'

Mary said, 'Found your vocation then?'

Chris replied, 'Yep, and here's my big news. I've left the Service. Had a meeting with the high-ups. They decided they could give me redundancy with "wounded in Service" benefits. So I can do this full-time. Love it!'

Ben slapped him on the back. 'I'm so pleased for you.' Then he thought of his daughter's blushes. 'Have you told Katy?'

'Going to see her tomorrow. She thought I was an arsehole when she first knew me.' He grinned. 'And I was.' He looked at

Ben. 'I'm hoping she might have changed her mind?'

'I think you're on a safe bet there.'

'And that you wouldn't mind…'

'Chris, my daughter is a grown woman and she knows her own mind. She's been winding me round her little finger since she was a tiny girl. If she's happy, then I'm happy.'

Ben felt Mary take his hand and squeeze it gently.

Chapter 13

Katy and Chris had arrived hand in hand. As soon as they were through the front door, Katy said, 'Dad, we're sort of going out.'

'Sort of?'

'Well, we're seeing how it goes.'

'Very sensible.'

'But we're here to tell you something you'll really want to know and, of course, to have a good feed at the same time. Where's Mary? Hope she's doing dinner. You're good but she's better.' And to soften the blow she reached up and kissed him on the cheek.

'You're in luck. She's in the kitchen.'

After hugs and kisses all round, Katy flopped into a chair and sighed. 'God, I'm working sooo hard. "A" levels were a doddle compared to this. But someone told me that Computer Science is much easier. She was bound for a 2.2 in Maths but changed to Comsci and got a First. I love the physics though so might go that way. If I live, that is.' She paused for breath and held her hand up. 'But, you lovely people, I have found time to look at your B.H.S clue and I think I have something to show you. But I'm going to make you all wait until you've told me about your wedding plans. Delayed gratification, remember, Dad? And please do not tell me I have to wear a floaty pink dress, cos if you do, I'm not coming!'

'No,' said Mary. 'Pink floaty dresses are definitely banned. Unless our menfolk want to wear one. That would make it memorable.'

Katy interrupted, 'Don't tell Henry. He might even do it. He has got a very good pink suit so that might suffice.'

Mary continued, 'It's going to be small and super lovely. We were thinking of having it at Ethel's now that Ben has come to terms with the bad things that happened there. But then we thought of Agnes and Josephine. We decided we couldn't ask Agnes to go back into the place where she was raped, and equally, couldn't ask Josephine to revisit anything to do with Stanley Murdock. We don't want Stanley looming over us in ghostly form.'

'Gruesome thought,' said Chris. 'And there's also Dobson being murdered there. Though his generous endowments have made him person-sort-of-grata again.'

Mary continued, 'As University Librarian, I get to visit all the colleges and we're thinking of Queens.'

'My old college,' said Chris.

Katy punched him. 'You never told me.'

'You never asked.'

'Anyway, Dad, when is it to be? You know I have a very full diary!'

'Outside term time and that's as far as it's got. And, Katy, we will make sure to time it so you'll be able to fit us in to your busy schedule. Now, dinner, I think.'

After the dinner where Katy declared herself 'stuffed', Ben asked, 'Are you too full of good food to enlighten us about your breakthrough.'

'Yes,' added Chris. 'She hasn't even told me yet.'

Katy delved into her capacious bag and pulled out two crumpled sheets of paper. She smoothed them and, when the corners wouldn't lie flat, placed empty wine glasses on them. On one page was written the clue from Knatchbull.

B.H.S. She owns it all, Tavela, Arcadia.

On the other was the names of the conspirators in alphabetical order.

Andrews, Asquith, Braybrook, Hutchinson, Ingleby, Overton, Sandys, Sheringham, Thornhill

'See it?'

They all looked at the pages and all shook their heads.

Ben could see that Katy was enjoying their incomprehension so he kept quiet. He suspected she wasn't going to make it easy for them. He was right.

'Give us a clue,' he said.

'It's nothing to do with who owns the shops and businesses.'

Mary asked, 'So the content of the words doesn't matter.

The Greens are surplus to requirements?'
'Yep.'
'And I've done all that work on their money and its movements! It was an eye-opener, I can tell you.'
'But wasted, I'm afraid.'
Mary looked again. 'Oh, oh, oh. I've got it.'
'Spill it out, Mary.'
'If you put the conspirators in this order, you get the first letters of the quote.' She wrote them down.

Braybrook
Hutchinson
Sandys / Sheringham
Sandys / Sheringham
Overton
Ingleby
Andrews / Asquith
Thornhill
Andrews / Asquith

'Now all we have to do is to work out what that order means.'
As Ben was about to speak, Mary's phone rang. She listened in silence. Then her face froze. Ben's immediate thought was of Henry, Mary's oldest and dearest friend. The conversation went on with Ben getting more and more worried. When he tried to intervene, Mary waved him to silence. She finished the call.
'Sandys has been found dead at his home.'
Ben's immediate reaction was one of relief. Their dear friend Henry would live to fight another day. His second thought was that he'd been wrong to suspect Sandys of being the Enforcer.
Mary was still talking. 'He'd phoned Asquith to apologise straight after the funeral and left a message on his answerphone. Asquith got worried when he couldn't get back to him. Asquith then phoned whoever his contact is in MI5 and they sent a tame policeman to investigate. Said policeman didn't think it looked suspicious but Parker decided to bring the body up from Devon so Jim Squires and his Home Office friend could do the post-mortem.

The body arrives today.'

Chris said, 'B H S – well at least we now know what the order means and who the next victim will be. We just don't know when, where or how. Anyone know anything about Sheringham?'

* * *

'Clever, this. He was on blood pressure pills. This was a huge overdose. And Brixham is a backwater so they'd probably have gone for "myocardial infarction" – heart attack in plain parlance.'

Ben watched as Jim Spire covered the body of Jonathan Sandys. Peter Shepherd, the man from the Home Office, nodded sagely. 'They don't see many murders down in Devon.'

Ben's fingers tingled. What was it about Devon? Something he'd read. He'd have to talk to Mary. Her sounding-board qualities were second to none.

Jim continued, 'He's got the red hand, same as the last one.' He uncovered Sandys' right foot to reveal precisely the same tattoo as had appeared on Hutchinson's foot.

Jim turned to Peter. 'I'm sure your bosses will want to know that. Any idea what we're to do with him now? No doubt they will be wanting to ship him somewhere.'

Peter looked at Ben. 'We're still deciding what to do. Can you keep his body for the time being? His brother is his next-of-kin and he's suffering from dementia so we can take things slowly while we decide what's best.'

'No problem,' said Ben.

'And you've no need to worry about IRA interference. We're sure they won't know where the body is.'

Ben was not at all worried about the IRA. Asquith thought it was an inside job and Ben was now beginning to believe this to be the case. He was as sure as he could be that the IRA were not implicated. But he had no idea who was involved or how desperate they were. His thoughts turned to Sister Theresa, the nun who had got in the way of a desperate paedophile. How many innocent bystanders might get killed this time? That was his worry.

Chapter 14

Ben and Mary were having a quiet dinner; a rare occasion these days as the house seemed to be in a state of perpetual motion. Ben relished this time alone with Mary and beamed across the table. Her rude response made him laugh out loud, something that was becoming commonplace after years of silence.

'OK, so you think Devon was important – any idea why?'

'Nope. That's where I hoped you might fill in the gaps.'

Mary shrugged. 'Duh. Think I'm a mindreader? Let's see if we can find a pattern. Hang on, I'll get the pudding.' She returned with two slices of vanilla cheesecake. Ben grinned. Mary's cheesecake made with real curd cheese would be enough to stop any attempt at conversation for a while.

Then Mary continued, 'This is what we think we know. First one died from choking on a sweet. And he was always sucking sweets. We believe it to be murder cos of the list – which only MI5 knows we have. The second, we know was murder, injection of adrenaline while he was sleep, and probably more than one perp. The third, overdose of his tablets, method of administration unknown, and would have been overlooked if it had been a one-off. We thought it was the IRA but they wouldn't know the order of murders so we've ruled them out.'

Ben added, 'But we do know they're mobilising for something.'

'Outside our remit?'

'Only if it's not connected to these murders and the Murdock plot. And that, we don't know.'

'But we do know that Sheringham is going to be the next victim. What are MI5 doing to protect him?'

It was Ben's turn to shrug. 'Round the clock discreet surveillance. That's it, and it's time-limited. I get the impression that MI5 are not too fussed. Maybe they'd like to see the back of all of them.' Ben sighed. 'To be honest, I'm not too fussed either. Except that some were coerced so were already victims. Take

Asquith; he wanted to spill the beans but was leant on to keep quiet. And we've got a serial killer on the loose. The problem is, they sometimes make mistakes and kill the wrong person.'

'So what would you do, if you were the killer?'

'Wait till the surveillance is withdrawn.'

'So what are you going to do?'

'Go back and see Knatchbull, I suppose. He knows who the Enforcer is. He won't tell me but he might give me an inadvertent clue.'

'He's MI5 through and through. Bet you a tenner you don't get anything.'

'You're on!'

* * *

Jeremiah Knatchbull was looking pleased with himself. 'So, Ben, you haven't cracked my clue. You had to come back to get more information. I'm surprised. I thought you were cleverer than that.'

'Jerry, you misunderstand. We've cracked your BHS clue. It puts the conspirators in a certain order. We believe it to be the order in which they are to be killed.'

Knatchbull sat up. 'Oh, that's interesting. Very interesting. Way off kilter, of course. Wrong, but interesting. It shows a certain amount of cleverness. I can't stand stupid people. How about you?'

One lie told, thought Ben. He replied, 'I deal with all sorts, some cleverer than others. Tell me, did your leader think you were stupid?'

'Ah, yes. He underestimated me. Our leader was a genius, an evil one. I think he underestimated everyone. It meant that he had contingencies for every eventuality.' Before Ben could ask more about the leader, Knatchbull continued, 'Maybe you're a genius but somehow I think you're not evil. Are you, Ben?'

'No, I'm not evil. Are you?'

'That's an interesting one. I don't think so. I had scores to settle, but ultimately I failed. You outwitted me. Our leader would have wanted you on-side. That's for sure.'

Ben already knew far more about Knatchbull's leader than he would ever confide to Knatchbull. That was his advantage and he wasn't about to give it away. He feigned ignorance. 'You've never told me who your leader was. He didn't appear on that video. Can you give me a clue to his identity? A name?'

'Moira.'

Ben managed to sound surprised. 'He was a woman?'

'Norman. That's all I'm saying. Crack that and you might find out who he was.'

Ben already knew about Norman's Bar in Moira, that little town in Northern Ireland where Stanley Murdock had lived. Ben had been there with Mary on their quest to find Tommy. He knew that Norman's Bar had been the haunt of Stanley Murdock while he'd been a British spy under cover in Northern Ireland in the eighties and nineties. Ben wondered how much of his murderous plot had been hatched there. He brought himself back to the present. 'That all? That tells me nothing. So, lets get back to the living; the conspirators who are still alive. I want to know who wants to kill them?'

'It was you who said someone wanted to kill them. I didn't. They're mostly ancient. Have some of them died?'

Ben decided not to answer that. 'If I'm to keep on visiting, I need to take something away. Tell me something about the Enforcer.'

'But I've told you something about our leader. Isn't that enough?'

'As I say, I'm interested in the living. They probably want to stay that way. The Enforcer?'

Knatchbull spent some time looking into space and fiddling with his tie before he answered. Ben waited, disguising his impatience, and the reply eventually came. 'I expect my obituary will have been in the Times. I hope they said good things about me.'

This supposed non sequitur confirmed to Ben that there had been a decision to systematically murder the remaining conspirators once 'the cake' had been demolished, and that Knatchbull's reported death would have been the trigger. And Knatchbull had known that.

'The Enforcer?'

Knatchbull straightened his tie and stood up. 'Next time,

Ben.'

'You think there will be a next time?'

'I hope so. Remember, it's what's keeping me alive.'

'OK. So how many lies have you told me today?'

'Just the one.'

'And is your last answer "the one"? Is that your lie? Because that would cause me some difficulty.'

'Ben, of course not. I have my code of ethics, you know.' He laughed. 'And I know which side my bread is buttered.'

Chapter 15

Ben had brought the four of them together to tell them about his meeting with Knatchbull. Mary, Henry and Katy were sitting snugly on Henry's voluminous settees in his study at Ethel's. They were drinking Henry's special g and t's. Henry had recently been converted to seaweed gin and, in turn, he'd converted them all. He had even tried to persuade Ben that, while he was in Devon, he could take a detour to West Wales to get some. Mary, in turn, had suggested that buying on-line might be a better bet.

After his first sip, Ben recounted the content of his meeting with Knatchbull. He finished by saying, 'He's playing with me – feeding me scraps. Testing my intelligence. But then, what else has he to do with his time.' He thought for a moment. 'But I'm sure he's hiding things in plain sight.'

'What d'you mean?' asked Mary

'There's more to what he says than meets the eye. There's always more meaning if only I can see it. And now he's said he won't talk if it's recorded at all, so I can't even take notes. I have to understand while I'm there or remember and analyse it all.'

'Well then, Dad. It's a good job you've got that photographic memory even if it is only partial.'

Mary said, 'We don't seem to have learnt much worthwhile from his words. They just confirm what we already know. What about what you've seen; body language, anything to be gained from that? Any mannerisms that related to particular topics? It's a long shot but it might help us know when he was lying.'

Ben leapt out of his settee nearly upending his drink in the process. 'Mary, you are one very clever woman. Of course. He touched his tie. Fiddled with it. It really annoyed me. But when I think back, it was only when I mentioned the Enforcer.'

Henry joined in. 'The tie? MCC or regimental. They'd be his fallbacks.'

'Not sure. But I can see it in my mind's eye. Blue with white feathers.'

Katy was already tapping away at her screen. 'I've gone for MCC first.' She showed it to her father. He shook his head. Then she tapped away again. 'Blue, you said. How about this one? Grenadier Guards. Blue with white plumes?'

'That's it,' said Ben. 'But all it tells us is that he still wears his regimental tie.'

Henry let out a great roar of laughter. 'Well it would do if that was his regiment! I know for a fact that he was Coldstream. Now I wonder if we can guess who was the Grenadier?'

Katy said, 'No idea. All it tells me is that he's not on suicide watch, otherwise no tie. Or, could be they want him to top himself and save them the cost of keeping him.'

Mary silently delved in her bag and brought out a crumpled ten pound note and handed it to Ben. 'You win,' she said. 'But you did need us to help you.'

* * *

When they got back home, Ben suggested that they look again at Murdock's final missive to see if they could join up any more dots.

Mary read it out.

If you are reading this, then our plan to rid the North of taigs has failed. We got some of them but the Fenian lovers in England will have won this time. But be warned, we just need a ripple in the fabric of peace and the forces will stir again. We've lost the battle but the war will continue. There will be an uprising and it will ensure that there is never, ever, a chance of the North being overrun by the left-footers from the South. As long as there are Ulstermen, there will never be a united Ireland.
I thought I'd settled it when I made sure that bloody interfering woman was killed. But she must have got a message through. They foiled us. Our man within couldn't stop them getting Blair elected. Pathetic. Outflanked by his own people. Someone in there knew – someone skewed the election. Never found out who.
Knatchbull is a lightweight. True to the cause but none too bright. He's been a useful shield but, without me, he'll eventually go under. He'll crack under pressure so I've only told him what he needs to

know.

But he doesn't know where these are; no-one knows. Even our Enforcer doesn't know. So how the hell did you find them? This will not end. The cake gets demolished and then there were Neele and the Colonel. No matter – but be warned. This battle's over but the war goes on. No surrender.

She tossed the letter away, squeezed Ben's arm and said, 'I'm so glad we never knew him.'

'Me too. And all that time ago, when his body arrived on my premises, I said what I always say when it's been a traumatic death, "We'll give you the dignity in death that you lost in life." Huh! Didn't know then that I was dealing with my wife's killer, and that he'd murdered many more. Oh, and also a rapist – did I mention that? We buried him with due ceremony. I didn't know that we were burying an evil man full of hate.'

'And what would you have done if you had known?'

Ben shrugged. 'I really don't know. I'd like to believe I'd have done the same, but maybe I'd have been like Alistair and spat in his face. Who knows? But what I do know is that we must do our damnedest to save the half-innocent from the tentacles that are reaching out for them from beyond the grave.'

'Yes, it does seem that some of them were foolish, maybe a bit arrogant – and certainly consorting with people way beyond their pay-grade. For that, they don't deserve to die. Then there's the innocents, the squaddies who were inveigled into Murdock's army. They need to be rehabilitated.'

Mary was interrupted as Ben's phone rang. 'Number withheld. Probably a cold caller.'

'Answer it. It may be important.'

Ben swiped up and put the phone on loudspeaker. Mary let out a cry. 'Oh no. That's dreadful.'

Ben responded, 'Either the Enforcer knows more than Murdock realised – and that's not likely, or it's just one more of Murdock's secrets.'

Chapter 16

'How did it happen?' Henry lowered himself noisily into his chair. 'Knees giving me gip when I sit down. Give me gip all the time but the worst is between standing up and sitting down. Mustn't grumble – still alive not like those poor souls.'

Ben waited until Henry had settled himself. 'It was the day before yesterday. Apparently, three of them have been meeting up every week. They went to the same pub and their wives said it helped them with the PTSD, anxiety, depression – whatever. All of them suffered some form of mental distress. They were coming out after their session – a bit the worse for wear – when a car mounted the pavement and all three were mown down. Not an accident cos the car reversed over one of them, then roared off.'

As Henry mopped his eyes, Mary took up the tale, 'It was a busy street and there were several witnesses. One took the car number but it was stolen and found later burnt out. Two others did first aid but all three died at the scene. Police have taken statements and they've got an E-fit of the driver and passenger. Look at these.'

Henry took the proffered papers. 'Well, blow me down. Clever what they can do these days. Better than the olden days when someone drew a picture which was usually basic and looked nothing like the perpetrator. These look like real people and I'd say these are a good likeness for those photos from Murdock's stash. Got them with you?'

Ben retrieved the two photos from his inside pocket. Henry heaved himself up and took the photos and E-fits over to the window. 'Oh, dear God. It looks like their job is to target the foot soldiers. Shameful, that. What does Parker say?'

Mary answered, 'We get the impression that MI5 isn't too concerned if the conspirators get hit. They'd do what they could to protect them but it wasn't a priority. Basically, they were implicated in the conspiracy and therefore carried some guilt. But now the poor bloody squaddies are being targeted, it's a whole new ball game.'

As Henry turned away from the window, Ben thought he

suddenly looked very old. Then he straightened his shoulders and pointed at Ben. 'We've got a job of work to do. How many are there?'

'From the list that we found in Murdock's box, more than two hundred ex-soldiers had been recruited to his army. We don't know how many have died, or decided to back out – if they had the option. We're assuming they're sleepers, waiting for the call to go back to Ulster to kill Catholics. And we don't know how the call was going to be made. MI5 is looking closely at the list to see if there are any clues there. Chris had already taken on the job of finding and rehousing those who've really fallen on hard times, but these three don't fall into that category. It seems they had a support network but they were still suffering.'

'Well, we'd better get the army to get its arse in gear to give these men the support they deserve.' Ben had never seen Henry so angry. 'Some of these will be hard men but, my bet is, most of them will be lost souls who the army spat out when they no longer needed them. Two hundred ex-army recruited to Murdock's murderous gang. That's not something our country can be proud of.'

Ben spoke. 'We need to talk to some of these foot-soldiers. I'll get on to Parker.'

* * *

Later that same afternoon, Ben and Mary were sitting in a riverside pub nursing pints of local ale. Ben mused, 'The Thames used to be filthy. All that shipping, till the docks closed, I suppose.'

A voice behind him joined in, 'Yeah, it used to stink to high Heaven in summer. Didn't stop us kids mudlarking though. One time I found some Roman coins. Then my brother sold them to a dodgy geezer and we split the quid between us. Thought we was rich.' He smiled, 'That was probably the first time in my life I was cheated. Not the last though and that's why you're here.'

The man hadn't finished his reminiscences. He looked round. 'The Gun used to be a grotty little pub – full of real workers. Look at it today, all ponced up. I thought I'd come back to the old stomping ground, see how much they'd prettied it. Used to go to school in Wapping. Would you believe it? Now they've got a Waitrose where my schools was. The nuns were ferocious, mind you, but we deserved it. You must be Ben and Mary.'

The man held out his hand. They shook hands solemnly. 'Nick Winter at your service.'

Ben looked over Nick Winter; expensive clothes, neat haircut, posh trainers, a body suggesting he worked out. 'Thanks for seeing us. You know we're here because you've had a warning. And we know you had problems when you left the army. How are you doing now?'

'Yeah. Got into trouble. Went inside. Then I found a good woman who's been the making of me. I turned into a lucky sod when I met her, I can tell you.' He looked straight at Ben. 'Can tell you're ex-service. We have this look.' He nodded his head towards Mary. 'I struck lucky. Same for you, by the seem of things.'

Ben nodded. 'Yes, I'm a lucky sod too.'

Mary asked, 'So when were you recruited into Murdock's army?'

'She don't hang around, do she? It was when I was inside. I was one angry young man. And I'd learnt how to kill. Another con gives me this phone number to contact when I got out. Said they'd see me right. So I gives them a bell and they gives me two hundred nicker and says if I sign on there'd be some more when I gets called up. Well, that must be more than ten years since and I ain't ever been called up so I've had to make me own way.' He grinned. 'Started doing up and selling motors. Now I've got a string of garages all over Essex. Live in Loughton – beautiful house, looks out over the forest. There's a lot of them dodgy geezers living near me but I'm legit now. Lovely wife, two kids. I'm in God's pocket, as they say.' Then he stopped. 'Was in God's pocket till I got this warning. Home office, special delivery. I've taken it seriously, hired a couple of heavies. And I've sent the wife and kids to stay with her mum. So it's just me and the minders. Was that OTT, d'you think?'

'No. I don't think so. Did the Home Office send you photos?'

'Yeah, said look out for these two.' Nick took out copies of the two photos that had come from Murdock's stash.

Ben handed over his card. 'If you see them contact me

immediately. Can you do that?'

Nick looked at the card. 'Undertaker, that's clever. Good cover for whatever it is you are now.'

'Thanks. So, this call-up, how's it to work?'

'They're going to run an advert for a month – that bit at the top of page one of The Sun. It would tell us how to join up. Funny really. Even after all this time, I still look.'

'So what's it going to say?'

'Well, it's going to start with "Your country needs you," like them Kitchener ads. You know, with that pointing finger. Then tell us where to go and what to do.' He half turned. 'See those two over there?'

Ben looked over at the two men sitting at the furthest table. They were big. They were very big.

'They're as soft as the proverbial until you rile them. Then they explode. You wouldn't believe how fast they can move. I should be okay with those two. If that's all, it's time I was going.'

Ben nodded. Nick smiled a rueful smile and stood up. He shook Ben and Mary by the hand. He motioned to his two man-mountains who rose with surprising grace. As they left, Nick turned back and held the two photos aloft. 'Get those bastards will you. I could do with getting back to a quiet life.'

Chapter 17

Mary leapt out of bed. Ben groaned, 'What time is it?'
      Mary ignored the question. 'My God, that man was an evil genius. He covered all eventualities; planned every step. He was the puppet master when he was alive and he's continued his control from beyond the grave. He's still orchestrating events. He hardly put a foot wrong – except a nosy undertaker got in his way. My God, I'm glad you didn't cross swords with him when he was alive.' Then she stopped. 'But Diane did. Ben, I'm so sorry.'
      But Ben hadn't heard any of this. Having looked at the alarm clock and seen 5.03, he'd turned over, put the pillow over his head and was now trying to get back to sleep.
      'Ben, this is important. I know how the next conspirator is going to be killed.'
      Ben groaned again and turned back towards Mary. He sat up and looked again at the clock to make sure he hadn't been mistaken the first time. It now said 5.04.
      'Go on.'
      'And Then There Were… It's the title of that Agatha book and it's based on an old rhyme. It was your Devon fixation that cracked it.' She scrabbled under the bed and retrieved her tablet. She dabbed a few times on the screen then turned it so Ben could read it:

Ten little Soldier Boys went out to dine; One choked his little self and then there were nine.
Nine little Soldier Boys sat up very late; One overslept himself and then there were eight.
Eight little Soldier Boys travelling in Devon; One said he'd stay there and then there were seven.
Seven little Soldier Boys chopping up sticks; One chopped himself in halves and then there were six.
Six little Soldier Boys playing with a hive; A bumblebee stung one and then there were five.

Five little Soldier Boys going in for law; One got in Chancery and then there were four.
Four little Soldier Boys going out to sea; A red herring swallowed one and then there were three.
Three little Soldier Boys walking in the zoo; A big bear hugged one and then there were two.
Two little Soldier Boys sitting in the sun; One got frizzled up and then there was one.
One little Soldier Boy left all alone; He went out and hanged himself and then there were none.

Mary pointed to the screen. 'We're on Seven. Ten choked on a boiled sweet. Nine was killed in his sleep. Eight died in Devon. Looks like the next one will be killed with a knife, machete or something sharp. And we know the next one will be Sheringham.'

Ben took out his phone. 'MI5 are watching Sheringham. We need to alert them to this.' He waited while the phone connected. He put it on loudspeaker and left a message which explained to Parker what they had discovered. He looked at his watch. 'We'll have to wait for an answer so I suppose I might as well get up and do some real work. I've got five invoices to send and two bodies awaiting attention.' But before Ben had moved, his phone buzzed.

Parker sounded wide awake and to Ben's mind he didn't sound surprised by their message. 'Well, Mr Burton, you must be psychic. I was going to phone you but you pre-empted me at what might be called an ungodly hour. You are too late, I'm afraid. John Sheringham went out before dawn this morning on his vintage motorbike, as was his daily habit. Our car followed at a discreet distance. It's very fortunate for us that, this time, we sent a car. Sometimes we send outriders. There's a sharp bend on his usual route. He revs up and leans right over at that bend then rights himself straight after. If he hadn't straightened up he might have got away with it. He wasn't in halves as your rhyme suggests. More like a quarter, three-quarters; beheaded. It was a wire across the road – but it was dark and before our people could investigate properly the wire or whatever had gone. Means the perp was around to clear up – and quickly too. Risky, that. Of course, the details won't get into the papers. Motor bike accident; old codger going too fast. Something like that. Send over the rest of that rhyme, will you?' Before Ben could answer, Parker continued, 'Of course, I'm much more worried about our other group of potential victims. What do you think we should do about Murdock's foot-soldiers?'

* * *

Mary, Ben, Katy and Henry had gathered in Henry's study. Henry sat down heavily. 'The previous three might all have been considered natural causes but this one is obviously murder. Either the Enforcer doesn't care or, as we hope, doesn't know that we have the list of conspirators so believes he can afford to take risks.'

Mary joined in. 'Difficult to make "chopped himself in half" look like an accident though.'

Katy asked, 'Do you think the Enforcer knows that Sheringham was being watched?'

Henry patted her on the arm and answered, 'Well, young lady, if the watchers were half as good as they were in my day, I'd say no. But we can't be certain. I do, however, think that he'll speed up whether or not he knows that we're on to him.'

'Why so?' Katy asked.

Mary answered, 'He'll be trying to get it over with. If you look at the rhyme, it gets harder to keep to the letter of it so it may be he'll have to improvise. He seems to know the habits of his victims. Overton is next on the list. My bet is, he's allergic to bee stings or whatever the active chemical is in them. Murdock would have checked all that.'

Ben said, 'He probably made a study of all their lives and habits. And, what's worse, he most likely enjoyed it – deciding the means of dispatching them as he thought necessary.'

While they'd been talking, Katy's thumbs had been on overdrive on her phone. 'He'll need an adrenaline auto-injector. Overton, he'll need two.'

Ben tapped the contact 'Car' on his phone and immediately got through to Parker. He quoted his codeword then relayed what they'd found. When he came off the phone, he had relaxed somewhat. 'They're already onto it. They've put a paramedic in with Overton. Apparently, he wasn't too pleased until they told him it might save his life. Then he agreed to co-operate. And he's allergic to all sorts of things – including bee and wasp stings.'

Mary grimaced. 'I think Murdock must be the most evil person I've ever come across. He decided all this so he could organise these killings to his satisfaction. Worse still, he added further instructions so he could still get these people killed after he was dead. What sort of a person does that?'

Ben answered. 'A total control freak, psychopath, sociopath, evil genius. One of those – or all of them. Look at the way he treated his family, coercive control off the scale. Look at the way he raped Agnes and tried to rape Josephine. But Murdock was thorough. What worries me more than Murdock's ten little soldiers, is that there is no mention anywhere in his effects that the foot soldiers were to be killed. I'm wondering if another evil brain is masterminding those killings. If it's not Murdock then who and why? And I don't know the answer.'

Chapter 18

Ben could see that Chris was in high spirits as he swept into The Flying Pig. Long John followed at a more sedate pace. Ben and Mary stood to greet them and Ben was delighted to see that Long John was looking even healthier than last time. He was walking tall, not shuffling, and had put on some muscle.

When Mary said how well he looked, his eyes twinkled as he told them that the doctor had signed him off. 'Said I were fighting fit. He did add I were in good shape, "for my age", but I've got enough puff to do me gardening so I'm not bothered.'

'So you're off to the big city to badger the army high-ups into giving you more support. How many are you seeing?'

Chris answered. 'Twenty or so.'

'D'you think they'll listen?'

Long John looked dismissive. 'Aye, they'll listen but will they cough up the readies? Who knows? But we'll do our best.' He pointed a thumb at Chris. 'Col has the financials, I'm the poor squaddie who fell on hard times but has picked hisself up with the help of this charity, so I got to be on my best behaviour. Got to look downtrodden and upright at the same time. Got to tell them I'm one of the lucky ones – not like them poor buggers in Murdock's army.'

Chris jumped in. 'You'll do no such thing. You shouldn't even know about that.'

Ben looked sideways at Chris, who shrugged in seeming apology. 'I got pissed one night and spilled the beans – just to John. I've told him that he must, on no account, tell anyone. And he's already told you!'

'Yebbut, they know already. So where's the harm?'

'Ever heard the term "careless talk costs lives." Well, that's careless talk.'

Chris looked stern. Long John looked downcast. 'Sorry Col. I'll be careful. But that man who helped save you – whasis name – he'll be there so he'll know about the secret army.'

'Yes, John Harris will be there. He's organising the bigwigs.

We won't know who else is in the picture so we must be circumspect. We'll let Harris lead and we'll follow.'

'Course, Col. I'll behave.'

Chris looked at his phone. 'Time we were going. Mustn't miss the train.'

As they left, Ben was wondering how many beans Chris had spilled to Long John and whether taking Long John along to sweet talk the army personnel had been such a good idea.

* * *

Knatchbull had asked for another meeting. Ben's first thought was that he was incarcerated alone with only his guards for company so he must be bored,. There were many in the spy community who would very much like to interview Knatchbull but Knatchbull had decreed that he would talk to Ben and to Ben alone, so boredom could not be his only motive. Much as Ben disliked being dependent on Knatchbull, he had to admit that he rather enjoyed the tussles of logic with him. He'd already decided that he must have a masochistic streak because he found the co-dependence both distasteful and energising. He'd discussed this at length with Mary. Although she had only met Knatchbull once, and that time she had been disguised as the downtrodden wife of an ex-soldier, she had repeatedly told Ben to be alert at all times. She'd told him that she did not think that he was in any physical danger but that Knatchbull might try to recruit him in some insidious way.

Knatchbull was, as ever, impeccably dressed. He wore a dark blue blazer with brass buttons polished to a high sheen and cream trousers. Instead of a tie, today he sported a blue cravat. Ben had 'dressed up' for the occasion, but felt dowdy in comparison. He wondered what Knatchbull's outfit was telling him today – and also what his dark suit was saying in return.

He opened his remarks with a question. 'How many lies today? Just the one?'

Knatchbull laughed. 'D'you remember that? "Just the one, Mrs Wembley." Must be twenty years. It'll be on DVD. Here's a favour you can do me. Ask them if I can have those DVDs.'

'I'll do that. But you haven't answered. How many lies?'

'OK, just the one.'

Ben pointed to Knatchbull's breast pocket. 'Yacht club badge? I hadn't thought of you as a sailor.'

'In my early days – but recently…' Knatchbull waved his arms at his surroundings. The bare walls of their meeting room seemed to draw in on them and Ben had to pinch himself to stop himself feeling sorry for this man.

'Sit down, I'll order tea.' Knatchbull rang a small bell, a soldier appeared and tea and biscuits were ordered. Hotel service, thought Ben. He wondered if this had been authorised. Knatchbull continued, 'You, my friend, are my ticket to freedom so I've got to keep you sweet but also keep you guessing.' He looked through the high window at the sky beyond. 'Maybe one day I'll take you out on the Solent. It's quite the most exciting thing – apart from spying, of course.' He adjusted his cravat, then patted his breast pocket. Ben noticed there was no handkerchief showing. Knatchbull continued, 'In here, I've had a great deal of time to cogitate. I've been thinking about my life. Now tell me, d'you think spying is addictive?' He didn't wait for a response. 'They say that Philby, Burgess and Maclean became addicted to it long after their passion for communism was spent. Terrible end to their ridiculous lives. Hated Moscow when they had to live there, but spied for Russia all their lives.' Knatchbull's eyes gleamed with an intensity that Ben interpreted as the zeal of a bigot. 'They got away with murder but I'm the one considered a terrorist. Is it fair? Of course not. I only worked for my country. I did what I thought was best, to keep the Kingdom united.'

This was the longest speech that Ben had heard – and the first time that he had seen emotion from this man. He revised his opinion. This outpouring was a display of anger and jealousy not zeal. But he had to find out if the zeal was still there.

'Do you think what you did was right?'

'Now there's the sixty-four million dollar question. Was I right? Remembering what happened to the Cambridge spies makes me wonder if any of it is ever worthwhile. At first I was consumed with hatred for the people who'd murdered members of my family. That was my vengeful stage. Then the double life became exciting; staying one step ahead of the clever brains in our department of state.'

'So that's why you'll talk to me and no-one else? I got the better of you.'

'I admire that – brains, genius maybe. You should have met our leader. He was an extraordinary man, ruthless and charming in equal measure. And devilishly clever. You would have got on – if your infernal moral code had let you.'

Knatchbull had never divulged the name of his leader. Ben decided it was time to show some of his cleverness. 'So Stanley Murdock was a genius?'

Knatchbull first looked startled, then let out a bellow of laughter. 'And I thought you were coming to see me to find out who our leader was. But, all this time, you knew about Stanley. Clever.' He rubbed his temple. 'So, now I'm wondering, what is it you really want to know?'

'You don't get any real news in here so I can bring you up to date on a few things. But if I do, I'll want something in return.'

'Seems like I deal I can live with. What can you tell me of the outside world?'

Ben knew he was walking a tightrope. Reveal too much and he would lose the initiative; reveal too little and he wouldn't get what he wanted in return. What he really wanted was the name of the Enforcer for he was as sure as he could be that the Enforcer was orchestrating the deaths of the collaborators and the foot soldiers.

'Tell me what was to happen if Murdock died before you.'

'Nothing. Stanley had laid out what we should all do and that was to cover our tracks as best we could and lie low. None of us knew that he had secretly filmed us. Careless of him to die and let that get into the public domain. Putting it in plain sight on the wrong DVD box was clever but obviously not clever enough. That was so unlike him. He should have known that his offspring might distribute his effects to charity shops after his death.'

This was the story that Ben had sold to Knatchbull. He was pleased that Knatchbull had bought it. The secret of the provenance of the recording, that it had come from Murdock's wife via Tommy, her next door neighbour and lover in Northern Ireland, was only known to a select few. And that few did not even include MI5. Tommy had done them all a great service and Ben was prepared to protect him from all-comers.

Ben knew he was giving out information beyond his question when he asked, 'And what was to happen if you died before the others?'

'Ah! So I'm dead, am I? Wasn't certain after your last visit but I thought they'd have put in the death notices. It's what I would have done. Good to know.'

'So what was to happen?'

'Nothing, that's what. I was expendable.'

Ben smiled inwardly. Either Knatchbull didn't know that his death was to have been the catalyst that began the killing of the conspirators or he was lying. But Knatchbull had given him the Arcadia clue so he had to know about the plan to kill them in sequence. Ben decided that the one lie had now been told and he decided not to pursue it.

'Sorry to hear that. It must have been galling for you not to have been appreciated.'

'You've got to the nub of it. I've had a lot of time to think while I've been in here. I've realised it's what drove me on. I was never good enough so I was always trying to gain favour.' He looked so downcast that Ben did begin to feel sorry for him. Then he remembered Mary's words. No, he was not going to be beguiled by this man.

Knatchbull continued, 'He knew that, of course, Murdock. He got inside your skin and used it against you. We were all in thrall to him.'

'Sounds like a cult.'

Knatchbull slapped his thigh. 'You've got it. That's exactly what it was like. And he's still controlling us from beyond the grave.'

Ben tried to look nonchalant. 'How so?'

'You know that already. You solved my clue.'

'You going to tell me about the Enforcer?'

Knatchbull looked directly at Ben. 'You're slipping. I gave you a clue almost as soon as you walked in. A whole lot of clues, actually. So no more. You'll just have to sift through your memories and see where it takes you.'

'We need to stop him. If it was like you say – a cult, then the conspirators don't deserve to die. Tell me some more.'

'Ben, you've shown yourself to be clever and resourceful. I've told you sufficient to get you what you want. Drink up your tea. I've enjoyed our chat but I think I've talked enough for today.'

'OK, but I have one last question. Why target the foot-soldiers? Surely, they really don't deserve to die.'

Knatchbull leapt up, knocking his tea cup to the ground. On the tiled floor, it smashed into a thousand tiny pieces. He ignored it as he paced the room. 'How many dead?'

'Three, so far.'

'That wasn't part of the plan. The Enforcer would stick to the plan.' He paced some more. Ben remained silent and still.

'It's got to be those others and you know who they are. Got those photos with you?'

Ben took out the four photos that had come from Murdock's box.

Knatchbull pointed. 'These two are dead.' He pointed again. 'You need to find these. Murdock could control them but it looks like they've gone rogue.'

'Names?'

'I never knew their names. They were Murdock's minders. He had some sort of hold over them.'

Ben's brain was in overdrive. What hold could Murdock possibly have had over murderous terrorists? Then links started forming. He asked, 'Did they ever mention a man called Jacko or a doctor in Belfast called Neville-Taylor?'

'Oh, they were in cahoots with Taylor, all four of them. Used to go on fishing trips with him.'

Ben clenched his fists and took a long, deep breath. He went to the door and knocked sharply on it. He turned to Knatchbull. 'Thank you, Jerry. I'll be back.' As soon as the door was opened, he strode out. He had to get out to the fresh air because he knew full well what these men had been fishing for, and it wasn't fish.

Chapter 19

'It's one of the last taboos. Clever old Murdock.' Henry held out his glass for a refill.

Mary took it and said, 'A weak one this time?'

'If I must.'

Mary, Ben and Henry had gathered in Henry's newly tidied and spring-cleaned rooms. The carpet still showed brighter patches where piles of papers had resided for several years. Now all had been sorted and archived by Mary with some help and more than a little hindrance from Henry. Ben looked round 'Do you still know where to find what you want?'

'Good Lord no, dear boy. I just have to ask Mary and she comes up with the right information. It's wonderful having a university librarian as an assistant, as I'm sure you know.'

Ben smiled at Mary. 'Yes, it is.'

Henry continued, 'And ditching a load of the old stuff has decluttered my brain. I've focussed in on Crimea. I thought that, after Georgia, it would be next in his sights. I fear I'm right.' He tutted. 'Politicians are so short-sighted.' He added, as if it was an afterthought, 'And your Irish felons of course. Got them on my radar. So, paedophiles, eh.'

'Parker's circulated the pictures of the two Glaswegians to all Forces but stipulated that the photos are not to be revealed to the press or public at present. He doesn't want those two going further to ground than they already are. He's told the police that they are suspected terrorists as well as paedophiles, so discreet information gathering is the order of the day. Sarah says being paedophiles has put them at the top of the list for action for your average cop. Higher even than terrorists. So we're hoping for sightings.'

Mary said, 'You've told me about the clues Knatchbull says he gave you at the beginning of your conversation, From what you've said, I can only think it was his boating gear. Remember, last time it was his tie – for the wrong regiment. He mentioned sailing on the Solent. Do you think he was referring to Andrews?

He owns a yacht. I think our next move will be to visit him.'

* * *

Before they'd had a chance to organise a meeting with Andrews, an urgent call had sent Ben and Mary straight to QE hospital in Kings Lynn. They hadn't checked, but were in luck, arriving just at the start of visiting time. They hurried through a maze of corridors and staircases. At last they saw a lone police constable sitting half way along a hospital corridor. She held up her hand as they tried to enter the small ward. 'Sorry. Got a list of who can go in. Names and ID needed.'

Ben and Mary produced driving licences and were checked off on a very short list. Ben wondered who had provided the list and his guess was Parker. Chris was no longer 'one of theirs' but he had been, until recently.

'Doctors say only ten minutes. Helps me if you could keep to that. Don't want them nurses giving me grief.'

Chris and Long John were lying side by side in a two-bed ward. Chris was in a better state than Long John. Chris could talk.

'Don't tell Katy. Not till we're looking better.'

Ben wondered if this was such a good idea. Katy's wrath at being kept in the dark was not something he would want for Chris in his present state. He decided that he would over-rule Chris and phone Katy as soon as they left the hospital.

Both Chris and Long John were looking battered and bruised. 'What happened?'

Chris pointed to the sleeping Long John. 'He saved my life. Hit and run. Car rode the pavement, hit a bollard, ricocheted off us then sped off. He pushed me out of the way. The bollard came off worst – and the car, of course.' Ben could see tears beginning to well in Chris's eyes. 'He took more of the force than me. I've just got a few cuts and bruises. He's got a broken arm and loads of soft tissue injuries. The docs say we'll live. It bloody hurts though.'

Mary reached out and squeezed Chris's hand. She continued to hold it as she said, 'He's a good mate to you. Trust the docs.'

'Yeah. He's a bit like the dad I never had.'

Ben wondered what was behind that statement but now was

not the time to ask. 'And now you owe him, just like we owe you. What can we do for you?'

'Catch the buggers that did this?'

Ben answered, 'What do the cops say?'

'They're on to all the local garages, plus stolen cars. They tell us it's joy-riders and they expect a burnt-out car and no arrests. Parker's taking it more seriously hence the list and ID.'

Ben spoke. 'You say "buggers". One person or more? Would you recognise anyone?'

'I think more than one, but I could be wrong. Joy-riders need an audience so I could be making that up. And no, it was too quick to see more than a blur. I can't even tell you the make or colour of the car – dark – that's all I remember.'

Mary joined in again. 'Where did it happen?'

'Middle of Lynn. Old roads, narrow, not the usual joy-riding scenario.'

Mary put on what Ben called 'her very serious face'. 'Do you think it was deliberate – like the squaddies?'

Chris replied, 'Thought of that. But that Glasgow pair don't know about us – me and John. They've obviously got access to Murdock's list of foot-soldiers but no way of getting intel on me. After I helped catch Knatchbull he's been very securely out of circulation so, even if he recognised me, he can't get the info out. You can be damned sure of that. So, I'm thinking we were just unlucky. Wrong place, wrong time.'

Mary persisted. 'What if you're wrong? What has Parker put in place for after your release?'

Chris grinned and then grunted. 'God, that hurts. Don't make me laugh whatever you do. You make it sound like a prison in here. He's giving me some minders until your two men have been dealt with.'

Ben noted the terminology – not 'caught' but 'dealt with'.

But Mary was on a different tack. 'You're assuming that, if it was targeted, you were the target. What if it was Long John? Is he getting any protection?'

Chris looked sheepish. 'Selfish git, aren't I? Hadn't thought of that.'

Chapter 20

Ben had hardly touched a dead body since Michael Murdock and Sarah's friend Pam had taken over the business. For over two years, he'd been off chasing the mess that Stanley Murdock had left in his wake. It was an enormous mess and, so far, it had enthralled him, exasperated him, nearly killed him. And it was a mess still unfolding. He knew that his motive now, in trying to bring it to a conclusion, was to prevent the slaughter of the innocents, those ex-soldiers and conspirators who had been taken in by Murdock's lies – or been terrified into obeying him and his Enforcer.

    He'd taken on the preparation of this body as a means of grounding himself again. As he washed and prepared for burial this ex-soldier, an eighty-five year old gentleman of the road, he wondered where his own future lay. He was pretty sure he would not end up living on the streets, as had this man, but he knew that a few twists of fate could turn his now-ordered world on its head. He too was an ex-soldier, and they were at high risk of a fall. He'd had a severe head injury and that, so often, resulted in depression. He'd suffered depression, on and off, since Diane's death and he had, for sixteen years, suffered from PTSD, another mental illness. With help, those demons were now in retreat. Bringing up his two girls had kept him reasonably sane in their growing years. And now he had Mary. Again, he thanked all the stars in the firmament that he had an anchorage to cling to. As if on cue, at that moment his anchorage appeared round the door.

    'Nick Winter's just phoned.'

    'Ah, Murdock's squaddie, the one with the big minders.' And, Ben added to himself, the one saved by the love of a good woman. He had a sudden thought. 'Is he OK?'

    'He's fine. Wanted to know if the two assassins were indeed paedophiles?'

    Ben laughed. 'Only the cops were told that. So, he has friends in the Met. What did you tell him?'

    'The truth, of course.'

'What was his reaction?'

'He just said, "Bastards" and hung up.'

'I hope he doesn't do anything stupid. He's turned his life around, and, if I remember rightly, he said he wanted to get back to his quiet life.'

Mary smiled, 'You give the impression that you want that too, but I'm not so sure.' She looked at the body lying on the slab in front of Ben. 'Nice job. He's beginning to look good. Will there be anyone coming to view him?'

'He had a couple of medals on him when he died. Michael's trying to find out his regiment so the Army can be represented at his funeral.'

Mary turned on her heel. Her parting shot was, 'Pity they didn't do more for him when he was alive.'

* * *

Four little Soldier Boys going out to sea; A red herring swallowed one and then there were three. To Ben, this suggested that the link with Knatchbull and the yacht club insignia must be Andrews. But Andrews had not been keen to see them. He had dismissed Ben's suggestion of a meeting by referring to his friends in high places in the Met who would look after him. There had been an arrogance in his tone that had left Ben fuming and wondering why he was putting himself out to help these people. The turning point in their phone call had come when Ben had suggested that a meeting with them might just be the additional factor that helped to keep him alive. It was at that point that Andrews' voice had wobbled slightly and Ben had seen through the bravado. Ben's anger had subsided as he'd realised that this man might just be terrified.

Andrews was residing at his club and would meet Ben and Mary there. He had suggested coffee at eleven which left Mary disappointed that they wouldn't be 'lunching at his club'.

They met in the foyer of a very exclusive club in Pall Mall. As they approached, Andrews sprang up from a low chair and jogged forward to greet them. He was tall and slim with a full head of sleek grey hair. His height and upright bearing, together with his abundant hair and show of agility, suggested to Ben that, had he been American, he might have been a perfect candidate for the presidency. They too seemed to need to show that they were still a force to be reckoned with.

Andrews ordered coffee then led them to a small room where they were the only occupants.

He opened the conversation in a staccato voice. 'You've heard about Overton?'

They had. Parker had informed them the previous evening that a swarm of bees had entered Overton's house by an uncapped chimney and that he had been transferred that morning to the intensive care unit at St Mary's Hospital in Paddington to be treated for the after-effects of anaphylactic shock. His adrenaline auto-injectors had saved his life. He was considered to be in a stable condition but they were taking no chances. The 'no chances' had included a brief press statement that he had died. Ben wondered if Andrews knew of the deception. It seemed that he did not.

Andrews gave a grunt. 'Poor sod. Another one of us has crossed the bar. And I'm holed up in here because it's safer than my home and the people who are supposed to be protecting us are doing a god-awful job of it. They've got some ridiculous idea that it's an inside job. Preposterous. Don't they know it's the Real IRA. Those bastards are popping us off one by one. The war is still on, you know. They haven't given up and nor should we.'

Ben decided to ignore this outburst. It suggested to him that Andrews had been one of the 'true believers' and had not been an unwilling accomplice in Murdock's plan. 'So, help us now to catch these felons. This may seem off-beam but humour me. You and Knatchbull – did you used to go sailing together?'

'Christ, no. Couldn't stand the man. Didn't socialise with him. Pretty useless, don't know why Murdock put up with him.'

That was not the response that Ben had been expecting. Had he got the sailing club clue wrong?

Mary joined in. 'Was there anyone else in your group that was a sailor?'

'Not that I know of. We weren't best buddies, you know. We had one job and one job only. We met only when we were called. Now we only meet at funerals.'

Ben knew this to be a lie but did not pursue it. He decided to come to the point. 'Who is the Enforcer?'

Andrews gave a hollow laugh. He waved his arm, taking in the magnificent architecture. 'If I knew that, do you think I'd be holed up in here? I'd be using the Enforcer for my protection. Better than the police. He got results.'

Ben could think of worse places to be 'holed up' but kept his counsel. He was glad that Katy was not here but was 'holed up' at Ethel's as he was sure she wouldn't have been able to keep silent about 'entitled white males'. The thought of Katy reminded him of her flight to Norfolk in reaction to news of Chris's accident. He was brought back to the present by Mary's question.

'Have they told you what they believe to be the means by which you are to be killed?'

'Their best guess is a boating accident so the yacht is out of bounds until those thugs are caught. They think it will be a re-run of the Mountbatten murder. They tell me they're keeping an eye on my boat. Not that it will do any good. Those Fenians are a devious lot. They'll manage to booby-trap it even if it is being watched.'

Mary gave Ben the pre-arranged signal that she thought they'd got all they could from this meeting. He agreed and, in truth, his desire to speak his mind to this bigot was becoming overwhelming. Time to retreat.

'Thank you, Mr Andrews. We'll see what we can do to help you.'

Andrews' last words cemented Ben's view of the man but added little to his knowledge. 'Captain Burton, it's Rear-Admiral Andrews, if you please.'

* * *

They were having a cup of coffee in less ornate but more acceptable surroundings. After a short walk for Ben to calm down, during which Mary had been silent and Ben had vociferously aired his views about bigots who continued to use their rank after they had left the services, they had found a small Italian coffee shop in a back street near Trafalgar Square.

As they sat down with their coffees, Mary spoke first. 'That was interesting, but I'm not sure how far forward it takes us. I do still believe that Knatchbull's nautical gear was a genuine clue. I'm just not sure what the clue meant.'

Ben was now thinking coherently. 'Tell me again what Murdock's clue about Andrews said.'

Mary took a paper from her bag and, as she retrieved it, Ben's eyes widened. He could see the butt of a small gun nestling among her other possessions. Maybe he didn't know Mary as well as he thought he did. To be discussed later.

But yet again she seemed to have read his mind. 'Henry gave it to me. The Lord knows how he managed to acquire it. It's the latest regulation issue for MI5 operatives in the field. Small and deadly. He thought we might need it one day.' She closed her bag, then ran her finger down the list. 'Now, the clue. Here it is,

'"Four little Soldier Boys going out to sea; A red herring swallowed one and then there were three."'

Ben groaned. 'A red herring, that could mean anything. So, it seems we're being misdirected about Andrews. We have a clue that is more convoluted than the others. We're no further forward and we've taken at least two steps back.'

'I think all we can do is make sure that Andrews doesn't get swallowed by a whale or eaten by a shark.'

* * *

As Ben turned the key in the front door, they heard the phone clicking to answerphone. He was too late to answer but heard the message.

'Nick here, Nick Winter. You said to get in touch if I had anything. I've got something. Meet you in The Grapes at four. Just the two of you.'

'So we're going to another gentrified pub in the East End. Owned by Ian McKellen.'

Ben turned to Mary, his eyebrows raised. 'How do you know these things?'

'Don't forget, I'm a university librarian. We read a lot.'

'And?'

'And Sergei and I used to meet there. It was off the beaten track.'

Ben was immediately solicitous. 'It might bring back painful memories. D'you want me to go alone?'

'It'll bring back memories no doubt – but if there is any pain, I can handle it. You might have to hold my hand.'

Ben smiled, 'My pleasure.'

Chapter 21

They were early, but Nick was already there. Ben immediately noticed that he was flanked by two new heavies, not the ones who had been at their last meeting. These two were smaller than the last pair but Ben would certainly not like to meet either of them in a dark alley.

Ben and Mary shook hands with Nick. The muscle-men took a step back in a co-ordinated move. Ben nodded his head towards them and said, 'New friends?'

Nick replied, 'My two best boys are on a very special job. You'll be pleased. Want a drink before we go?'

'Go where?'

'My lock-up. We can walk. It's a nice day. Let's just go and we can have a drink to celebrate afterwards.'

It was then that Ben looked round and realised that Mary was not beside him. One of Nick's henchmen pointed and said in a thick Eastern European accent. 'Her, she over there.'

He turned round but couldn't see her. 'There,' he pointed. 'She go in. She round bend.'

Mary was sitting at a table in the corner hidden from view. She was crying quietly. She smiled up at him through her tears. 'I'm OK. This is where we used to sit. Always vigilant. Ben, I've realised something. Coming here and seeing it all again. I have to make my peace with Sergei. I'll need to visit him in Ukraine before we get married. Is that OK?'

He sat down and took her hands. 'Of course it is. We all have to make peace with our past. I remember Josephine telling me I had to face my demons and now I've laid them to rest. We'll ask Henry how you should contact him. And you know that I'll help in any way I can.'

'Thank you.' She stood up. 'You're a good man. I'm not sure I deserve you.' She shook herself. 'But first we have to sort out this mess. What's Nick got to tell us?'

'He's taking us to his lock-up. I assume he has something to show us.'

The 'lock-up' was not a shed or garage. It was a penthouse flat in one of the converted warehouses that fronted the Thames near Wapping Old Stairs. They entered the building by a series of locked and alarmed doors and rose to the top floor in a super-fast lift.

When they exited the lift, Nick rang the bell on the only door – three short, one long followed by three short again. The door was opened by one of the original minders.

'Hi boss.'

'How has he been?'

'Quiet as a sleeping babe. You can tell he's a pro. They know when they're beat.'

Ben and Mary were led into an enormous room with floor to ceiling windows showing a vast vista of the Thames and beyond. For a moment Ben was enthralled by the view. 'Wow! This is amazing.'

Mary was more practical. 'Nick, do you own this?'

Nick grinned. 'The whole building. Listen, it's a great story of the little man making good.' He motioned them to a large settee and asked one of his minders to bring tea. 'Sit down and I'll tell you a bit of my family history. My many times great-granddad came over to escape the famine and settled in Wapping. There used to be a great little Irish community here. I loved it. The family grafted – mostly navvies. Anyway, just before the docks closed, two derelict warehouses came up for sale.'

Ben was smiling inside as this tale unfolded. It was not the content but Nick's accent that amused him. The over-the-top cockney tones had disappeared and been replaced by Nick's version of received English. Obviously, he no longer wanted them to think of him as a wide-boy car salesman from Essex.

The tea arrived in large bone china mugs. Ben was reminded of Agnes and her 'good, strong Irish tea – not the dishwater they serve over here'. He hadn't seen Agnes or Josephine for a while. They were only in Hunstanton. They'd have to go and visit soon to see how they were.

Nick continued, 'My dad was an entrepreneur. I must get that from him. He could see the potential so he persuaded his brothers to put in all their savings. Mind you, they had to be persuaded over a pint or two of the black stuff. Anyway, it paid off. They bought both the warehouses and sold the other one to developers when Wapping became a "bijous place to live".' His air speech marks and wrinkled nose told them that he was not enamoured of the gentrification of his birthplace. 'They spent the money on doing up this one, and my uncles had no children so it all came to me.'

Ben looked at the sparsely furnished surroundings which managed to look both modern and surprisingly opulent. 'D'you live here?'

'Nah. Hate it. Rent it out to mega-rich tourists. When we lived in each other's pockets, there was a buzz. Now, there's no community here. We've got a farm in Essex. Small village, better for the kids. It's a money-pit, mind you, but we love it.' He stood up. 'But I didn't bring you here just to listen to my family history. Come and see what I have for you.'

He led them along a corridor to what Ben assumed to be a bedroom. He noticed the heavy door, surely too sturdy for a normal internal door. It had two deadlocks with keyholes, a spyhole and a card entry system. Ben looked quizzically at Nick.

Nick responded to the unasked question. 'The very rich like to have somewhere safe to keep their valuables.'

They stood back while one of the muscle-men unlocked the door and entered the room. He called back to them. 'All OK, you can come in.'

The room was bare except for a heavy chair and a single bed. A muscle-heavy man was seated in the chair. His face was a mass of swellings and bruises.

'Well, well,' said Mary. 'If it isn't one of our Glasgow mercenaries.'

Ben noticed a slight change of expression on the face of the man sitting in the chair. It was indeed the face of one of the villains whose photo he held in his pocket, although the face in front of them was almost unrecognisable.

The man spat on the floor and responded in a broad Scottish accent, 'A'm no a mercenary.'

Nick's biggest henchman retrieved a mop from a bucket in

the corner and silently mopped the floor. 'He's a filthy bugger. Doing a dirty protest but we just keep cleaning him up.' He turned to Ben. 'We'll be glad to be rid of him. We have our standards to maintain.'

'And the bruises?'

'He gets a bit unruly when we try to clean him.'

Ben moved a little nearer to the seated man. 'I can't see anything, but I gather he's restrained in some way?'

Nick took a small keypad from his pocket. 'Newest gizmo. Not legal. He gets a shock if he tries to get out of the chair.'

'Aah. It's a good job I didn't hear that. And Mary didn't hear it either. Sudden and momentary deafness – it's a bugger – must get it seen to. What about how you caught him? Do we need to be a little hard of hearing about that as well?'

'Best you don't ask. When we knew he was a nonce – suffice it to say that we set a trap. We were hoping to get both of them but he came alone. So, when he doesn't return home to his bug-infested abode, the other one will be on his guard. Sorry about that.'

Ben took out his phone.

Nick pointed to it. 'Won't work in here. You can get a signal in the sitting room.'

Ben moved towards the door. 'I'll organise his removal. I think just tying him securely to the chair would be a good idea. The removal men will be here quickly once I've phoned.'

Chapter 22

'He's not talking. But then, we never thought he would.' Parker raised his hands and his eyebrows in synchrony. 'Any ideas?'

Ben thought for a moment then mimicked Parker's gesture. 'Not a clue. Well, not much of a clue, but we do have an idea. He's a hardened pro and if all your tricks haven't got him to talk, we are no further forward – except we've taken one paedophile terrorist off the streets. Have we got a name for him yet? And can you tell me where he is now residing?'

'No name. We're calling him Jimmy. And he's in the same place as Knatchbull. There's room for twenty there so we decided that two wouldn't constitute overcrowding. We're keeping them apart, of course. Separate guards, separate everything. They won't know the other one exists.'

They were sitting comfortably in Parker's office. Ben could see that two of Parker's grey men were quietly doodling on their notepads. The other was staring into space.

Mary had been sitting equally quietly. She had been writing notes. Now she looked up. 'Has he been checked for bee stings?'

'Yes. Nothing. We thought we had him for that but they turned out to be bed bug bites.'

Mary continued down a different track. 'We've talked to Dr Clare.' She turned to Parker's three wise men who were looking perplexed. 'Josephine Finlay's therapist. A forensic psychologist.' The three were still looking perplexed. Mary continued, 'Josephine Finlay? Murdock's killer? The woman who unwittingly brought this whole conspiracy out into the open.'

The grey man to the left of Parker hit his forehead with the palm of his hand. 'Sorry. Of course. That all seems such a long time ago.' He shuffled his doodles. 'And how is Ms Finlay?'

Mary replied, 'Dr Clare was instrumental in bringing Josephine back from the world she inhabited to the world of our shared reality. Ms Finlay is doing fine.'

Parker asked, 'How do you think we should use Dr Clare?'

Ben's admiration for Parker grew. This man was prepared to take risks. It was further enhanced by Parker's response when Grey Man Number Two said, 'We know nothing about this man. We need to investigate him.'

Parker's reply told Ben a great deal about Parker. 'Did anyone say Dr Clare was a man? I happen to know that she is a very competent practitioner and we have been paying her to look after Ms Finlay for some time. This is courtesy of our own former employee who, if you remember, nearly died while helping to catch Knatchbull. He's now recovering from a hit-and-run in Norfolk. Accident prone, that boy.'

Ben laughed. 'And Chris thought he'd pulled the wool over your eyes. He told me no-one within the service would know that they were paying for Josephine's very expensive stay at the Friary.'

Parker smiled. 'It takes very delicate wool to cover my eyes. And even with eyes uncovered, I might decide not to notice.' He added quietly, 'As with your Irish friend.' And Ben definitely saw one of Parker's eyelids sink slowly and almost imperceptibly. Ben was suddenly very thankful that Parker was on their side.

Parker then continued at a brisk pace. 'Chris has many admirable qualities but delicacy is not one of them. He's young and he's learning diplomacy. And he's got Long John, though I'm not sure how diplomatic that man is.'

Ben was amazed and aghast. 'How do you know all this? We didn't tell you.'

'Fingers in pies, dear boy.' Ben smiled again. It could have been Henry talking. 'Now, your Dr Clare, what does she say.'

* * *

It had taken some persuasion. The Grey Men had been aghast. But it seemed that only Parker had the power of veto and he had decided to endorse their strategy. It was now up to Ben to persuade Knatchbull – and he had few bargaining chips to play with. He sat once more in the austere visitors' room in this hidden prison and it dawned on him the Knatchbull was showing remarkable resilience. Ben wondered, if the situation were reversed, would he still manage to remain sane in here. He decided it was in the balance.

Knatchbull was late, as usual. As Ben sat waiting for him to appear, he decided that flattery would be a good starting point. This time Knatchbull had reverted to a smart suit. It was sombre black and he wore a black arm band and tie. Ben decided not to remark on his funeral attire, though he was sure that it had a meaning.

'Jerry, you're looking healthier each time I see you.'

'Thank you. I'm keeping fit and have turned a corner in my thinking. I'm hoping to use you as a sounding board for that. Now, you asked for a meeting. That's unusual, so I gather there are some developments. Apart from poor Overton, that is. I read the short obit in the Financial Times.' He pointed to his attire. 'Hence the black. Now what can I do for you?'

'We haven't yet cracked your yachting clue. It was a clue, wasn't it?'

'Yes indeed. Glad you spotted it.' He smiled broadly. 'So I'm keeping you on your toes. Good. I'll see if I can add a bit to point your feet in the right direction. Let me see.' He stroked his chin. 'It's to do with the Enforcer and the rhyme. That should move you on a pace. Is that what you came for?'

'That's helpful but no. That's not what I came for. I have a proposition for you. It could help your case. You want to get out of here one day?'

'Ah yes. You know that I do.' Knatchbull looked wistful. 'I'd like to go to the opera again before I die. And visit a Shaker village in New England. That will do me.'

Ben decided to go with the flow. That way, he might learn the best way forward with Dr Clare's strategy. 'I can see that you would want to go to an opera, it's bold, flamboyant and expensive, but a Shaker village? I would think that would be at the opposite end of the spectrum.'

'You're right. Opera is all extravagance. Shaker is simplicity. But one can appreciate both, don't you think?'

'I'm sure we can. I just don't see you and the simple life being soulmates.'

'Well, that's to do with my corner turning. Plenty of time to think in here. I've realised that religion is at the bottom of all that led to my present predicament. It ruined most of my life. No, that's not quite true; religion and my reaction to it ruined most of my life.

I was brought up to be very high church. The irony is, we were called Anglo-catholics. When Louis was killed by the IRA, who were supposedly Roman Catholic, I couldn't handle it. They were supposed to be pretty much the same as me and they'd killed my dearest relative. And so my vendetta started.'

Ben interjected, 'I get it. I can see how you, just a boy, could be conflicted by that.'

'Yes. If I'd had a therapist at the time, I'm pretty sure they could have sorted me out. I was a lost boy. Louis had been a strong influence; he'd looked after me.'

Ben could see the anguish on Knatchbull's face. Knatchbull continued, 'I've been reading up on him since being in here. I didn't know Louis had a dark side because I never saw that side of him. And when Stanley Murdock came along, I saw Louis in him. You know, the strong, charismatic man who knows what he wants and has the ambition to get it. I fell for it twice and look where I've ended up.'

If this conversion was true, and that was a big 'if', Ben's job had been made a whole lot easier. But first he had to probe more deeply. 'Where do the Shakers come into this?'

'I've been reading about them. There's got a well-stocked library here and they get me anything I ask for – as long as it's vetted by them. I came to the Shakers through the Quakers. If I ever get out of here I plan to become a Quaker, if they'll have me.'

'Jerry, I'm astounded. Is this a Damascene conversion? How can I tell if you're telling the truth or a pack of lies designed to pull the wool over my eyes.'

'You can't. You're going to have to trust me. Now, tell me about your proposition. You never know, it might be a win, win. What do you want from me?'

Chapter 23

Ben was sitting comfortably in Henry's study. Mary had poured drinks for the three of them and he noticed that they were considerably weaker than had been Henry's 'special g and t's' in the past.

Henry held out his glass towards Mary. 'I know you're trying to keep me alive but this is just tonic with no gin. How about pepping it up with some angostura? Then it might just be palatable.'

Mary carefully added three drops of bitters. 'Try that.'

Henry's face took on a mulish look. 'I should never have told you what that doctor said, then I could have continued with my riotous living.'

'Henry, don't be so intransigent. We're trying to look after you.'

Henry looked sheepish. 'I know. Everything slows down and then all your stuffing starts to fall out. Old age is a bugger. I suppose that's why Winston said we had to "keep buggering on". He lived to be ninety and they probably watered his whisky so I suppose I can't complain.'

'There you are then.' Mary pointed to the empty chair. 'I thought Katy was going to join us?'

'Well,' replied Henry. 'She was, until a so-called urgent call from Chris. He and Long John are being discharged from hospital and she had to be there to help them settle back in. Apparently, men are so bad at organising and looking after themselves, that they have to have a woman to do it for them. I tend to agree with her but I wasn't going to give her the satisfaction of saying so. Anyway, she'll be back the day after tomorrow.'

Ben smiled. 'It's wonderful not to have to worry about her. These days, I don't know what she's doing most of the time. When she lived at home, I'd be pacing the floor until she arrived home. Now I'm in blissful ignorance and can let her live her life any way she wants to.'

Mary responded, 'But you were ill then. And now your

PTSD is so much better. Henry, did you know that Dr Clare has discharged him?'

Henry took a sip and pursed his lips. 'Aaah! Your lovely Dr Clare. Now there's another admirable woman. So, you say he's game to play his part in her plan?'

'Hook, line and sinker. But, this Quaker stuff, I'm not sure we can trust him.'

Mary looked scathing. 'Of course we can't trust him. That's why we must have the bugs in place. Did you tell him they were going to be the same as the ones that you were wearing when we caught him?'

'I think that's one of the things that swayed him. He wants to see how we managed to fool him.'

Mary looked thoughtful. 'It's a big risk, letting the two of them talk to each other. But, I suppose, more of a risk for Knatchbull than for anyone. If he messes up, he stays in there till the Services have sorted out what they want to do with him. For the Glasgow One it makes very little difference. They'll never let him out so he may just decide to keep his secrets to himself. We know Knatchbull is good at what he does because it took a clever plan and a great deal of luck to catch him. Now we have to wait to see if he's as good a spy as we hope he is. Any idea how he's going to play it?'

'He's saying "softly, softly", gaining trust. I can understand that but we need answers fast. While the other Glasgow killer is out there, Murdock's foot soldiers are at risk. And while the Enforcer is out there, everyone is at risk.'

'When will the first meeting take place?'

'Tomorrow lunchtime. We'll get to hear them in real-time and transcripts pretty much contemporaneously.'

* * *

'So much for "softly, softly"! Did we get anything out of that?'

Ben, Mary and Alison Clare had listened to the first conversation between Jeremiah Knatchbull and the man they had named Glasgow One. Then they listened again, putting the recording on repeat. After the third time, Dr Clare was nodding to herself and Mary's gaze was focused at some point beyond the horizon. It was Mary who answered, 'Hush up Ben, we're thinking.'

He went to make some tea and left them 'thinking'. The set-up for the meeting had been decided by Knatchbull. The two inmates of that hidden prison would be allowed to have lunch together and their guards would be out of earshot.

When the two had met, each had seemed wary – but it was hard to tell with just the soundtrack. The introductory dialogue had confirmed that they had met before. The conversation had been banal and it was only from the transcript that Ben had been able to ascertain precisely what their man, Glasgow One, had said. Knatchbull had immediately suggested that they were being bugged and they should be careful. The facts that had emerged were thin. They had met twice before in Murdock's company. They had referred to 'the leader' and not by name. Both had been fulsome in Murdock's praise though the terminology used by G One had been courser. Apart from these two previous meetings, the two had not been in contact. Knatchbull had suggested that they should ask if they could walk in the grounds together.

When Ben took the tea through, Mary and Alison were still silent. Alison spoke into the silence. 'I need to see them. All psychologists know that much of communication is non-verbal – some people say it's over ninety per cent. I wouldn't put it that high but it is important and does add to understanding. We're getting words and tone of voice here but I really need to see them together. Is that possible?'

'Should be. There's a two way screen onto the visiting room. When I first met Knatchbull, he insisted that we met out of its line of sight. After that we met in the dining room where there's no covert surveillance. They stationed a guard at first but I knew he'd speak more freely if we were alone so they agreed to leave us à deux. I'm sure we could arrange it for one visit but after that, it's Knatchbull's choice and I think he'll try to get G One outside.'

Ben asked if they should let Knatchbull know he was being watched and Alison vetoed that immediately.

* * *

The next morning, Ben, Dr Clare and one of the more senior prison guards were sitting behind the two-way mirror in the small viewing area adjacent to the visitors' room. They had wanted Mary to join them but that had not been allowed. Ben would have pursued it but Mary had insisted that it was not necessary. Alison was the expert and Mary felt that she could not add to the equation so why clutter up the viewing room. The excuse for moving the two inmates had been that the dining room had to be painted. Ben's remembrance of it was that the paintwork was perfectly adequate. The smell of fresh paint was wafting to their nostrils and Ben assumed that the two they were about to watch could smell it too. Ben wondered who the painters were and surmised that they would be some of the guards. He hoped they had found some who were adept at diy.

Alison sat at the front and had suggested that Ben and the guard sit behind so as not to distract her. She had a pad and pencil and chose a stool to sit on. Ben sat behind and made sure he was comfortable so he wouldn't have to move. Knatchbull entered first and nodded towards the screen. He was looking particularly dapper in a crisp white shirt and yellow cravat. He carried a yellow striped blazer over his arm. He placed it carefully on the back of a chair and sat down. G One arrived a few seconds later making rather more noise than his companion. He was wearing a grubby hoodie and jogging pants.

Knatchbull looked him over. 'Hello again. You look rough. They treating you all right?'

G One grunted something unintelligible. Knatchbull continued, 'They'll do your washing, you know. And if you give them your size, they'll order clothes for you. I got them to bring me my favourite catalogues and I'm spending their money like water. You should do the same. It passes the time.'

'You'se bugged?'

'Good God no. Want to check?'

'Yeah.'

G One picked up the jacket and searched it thoroughly. Then he patted Knatchbull down in such an efficient manner that it suggested to Ben that somewhere in his background, he'd been taught to do this properly. Ben wondered how Knatchbull was coping with the bugs carefully placed under his penis and between the cheeks of his buttocks. Ben remembered them as being embarrassing but not uncomfortable. 'There'll be bugs in here, ye ken.'

'Oh, undoubtedly. That's why I've asked if we can meet outside. No names, no packdrill in here – yes?'

'Aye. You ken where we are?'

'Not a clue. But they know a lot about us so I'm thinking it's not an ordinary prison.'

'They ken what we were doing?'

'I suspect so but I've refused to talk. You should do the same.'

'Aye. I will. I was picked up by twa heavies who were none too gentle wi' me.' He pointed to his cheek. 'See the bruise. Tha' were them.'

'How are they treating you here? They've left me alone since I refused to talk.'

'The same. You'se the first person I've talked to since I've been here. Are there more of us in here d'ye think?'

'I don't think so. But who's to know?'

'Wonder if they've picked up ma boss?'

'You mean the Enforcer?

'Hush your rattle. D'ye ken who he is?'

Knatchbull turned to face the viewing screen. 'I saw him a couple of times but was never introduced. I'd know him if I saw him again but apart from that, I have no idea.' He shrugged, then turned to the other man, 'How about you?'

G One smiled an ugly smile. 'Well, tha' s for me to know.'

Knatchbull looked at his watch. 'Lunchtime, I think. I wonder where they'll serve it? We may be confined to our cells while the paint dries. I'll ask if we can have lunch together but I think they'll say no.' He turned and winked at the viewing screen and rang the bell by the door.

* * *

The guard hurried off to ensure that Knatchbull's request was turned down and the lunches would be served separately.

Ben looked disappointed. 'Well, that was short and sweet. Did you get enough?'

Alison riffled through her notes then replied, 'Oh, ample. Confusing at first but it soon settled down. Knatchbull is very clever. His Scottish companion less so.' She pointed to the empty screen. 'Your Scotsman is wary but not, I think, of Knatchbull. So their meeting outside might bring some useful information. And, either Knatchbull is a very accomplished liar or he's being truthful.'

'Hang on. He specifically said, to camera, that he didn't know who the Enforcer is. If that's true, then he's been playing me for a fool all this time. For weeks, he's been handing out little clues about the identity of the Enforcer for me to try to untangle.'

'Of course he has. Ben, you were his lifeline and he knew exactly what you wanted. He decided that his ticket to continued life was to string you along. You'd have done the same.'

Ben had to admit that she was right. He would have done precisely the same. 'So why the change of tack now?'

'Now, he has another lifeline. If he can get useful info from the Scotsman, which helps to wind up this case, he may well survive long enough to leave here. And remember, he said he'd be able to identify the Enforcer. That's his trump card. I'll write up my notes for whoever it is you're working for, but my first impressions are that Knatchbull knows which side his bread is buttered…' She smiled. 'And he doesn't want it to land butter side down.'

Chapter 24

As Ben paced up and down, Mary continued with her knitting. She held it up and looked satisfied. To his mind, the aran sweater was fearfully complicated, but she seldom seemed to refer to the pattern. He couldn't imagine how she could keep all that complexity in her head. She put down her knitting as she spoke. 'Nearly finished. It should be ready for your Christmas present. Remember to look surprised when you open it.' She patted the chair beside her. 'Ben, you're like a caged animal. Either sit down or go and get on with something else. They won't be meeting for another half hour.'

'I know. But we're on the brink of a breakthrough with the Enforcer. We need it. We've had nothing from Parker except that the conspirators are pretty much under lock and key. The foot soldiers have had another alert with one of the Glasgow Two still at large. I just hate waiting with nothing to do.'

'Go and phone Chris. Tell him we'll be out to see him soon to view progress on his project. See how he and Long John are recovering from the accident. If Katy's still there, you might even be able to have a chat with her.'

He was back within ten minutes. 'They're ok but they've had a break-in. The local cops think it was kids, but Chris thinks it was professional. All the cash and their shiny new computers have gone. Luckily they had back-ups of everything. A nuisance though.'

'And Katy?'

'She started back this morning. I'll try ringing her now.' He wandered off into the other room but was back within two minutes. 'Going to voicemail. I didn't leave a message. I'll try to get her later. There's a pile of invoices for me to check, so I'll get some work done.' He smiled. 'Though Michael and Pam really don't need my input any more. I believe I'm redundant but they don't want to tell me. Have they said anything to you?'

Mary put down her knitting. 'They haven't said anything but I think they've got the whole burial business pretty much under control. You're still the person a lot of people want to see leading the funeral cortege – those who've dealt with you in the past – but I think you could be redundant in the near future. So, when that happens, what are you going to do with your time?'

'We could have more holidays?'

'Or we could do more work for Parker? You know we're good at it.'

Ben looked sceptical – but not as sceptical as he had the last time she'd mentioned it. He was beginning to think that his desire for a peaceful life had been mixed up in his PTSD. Maybe peace wasn't what he needed. He didn't have to answer Mary's question as the alarm went off to tell them that it was time to start listening to Knatchbull and Glasgow One. They picked up their earphones and put them on. They could hear Knatchbull loud and clear. 'I'm walking towards the meeting site. It's the exercise yard attached to our secret hideaway. Ben, I hope you'll forgive me for stringing you along but meant what I said yesterday. I'll try to find out who the Enforcer is. Oh, he's coming. Over and out.'

For ten minutes, Ben and Mary listened intently to talk that was inconsequential to them but was helping to build trust between the two prisoners. Much of the talk was about whether they could be overheard and Knatchbull had offered to be frisked again but Glasgow One had said it wasn't necessary. After ten minutes, the conversation turned to the past.

Knatchbull said, 'I miss it. We had a purpose, we had a leader to take us there, we were moving towards our goal. I do hope the others are carrying on without us. Are they?'

'Aye, kind of. The leader's orders are being carried out. The Enforcer's doing one job and there's two of us doing the rest.' There was a pause. 'There was two of us. Now ma mate'll have to finish our job on his own.'

'He was clever, our leader. He compartmentalised.' There was another pause. It was obvious that 'compartmentalised' was not in G One's vocabulary. 'He gave people particular jobs that the others didn't know about.' Knatchbull continued, 'I was high up in the chain of command but I didn't know everything that you and the Enforcer were doing. Still don't.'

'Ach! We did the dirty work. Four of us under the command of the Enforcer. Only one left now.'

'What's the job now? Will he be able to finish it?'
'The job now is to mop up. Not leave anything to be found.'
'Ah, I see.'

Mary and Ben could see too. They knew it was a one-way connection so could voice their fears. Mary thundered, 'So it's on Murdock's orders that, if it goes belly-up, everyone is to be killed. Those poor bloody foot-soldiers, victims of the army, then victims of Murdock, then to be bumped off in case they know something they shouldn't.'

Ben gave Mary a hug, though he realised that he was equally angry at the injustice of it all.

Knatchbull was still talking. 'That's tidy. Knew the leader wouldn't leave any loose ends. See, I knew the leader because he was my commander, but I never knew the Enforcer. You must know him though, as he's your commander.'

The other man laughed. 'Aye, you'd think so. In the old days we'd get instructions by a man coming to the door. Always someone different, someone we didn't know. Then WhatsApp changed everything. We get our orders by WhatsApp. We do what we have to then cash is paid into our bank accounts. Comes from the Cayman Islands and who the feck knows where they are? No win, no fee keeps us on our toes. We've never met the Enforcer. We di'na know who he is.'

Glasgow One was not to know that this last sentence may have signed his death warrant.

* * *

The expected phonecall from Parker carried more bad news. A knife attack outside a pub in Skegness had left one of the foot-soldiers in a life-threatening condition. At first, it was thought that he could just have been unlucky, as knife attacks were not unknown outside that particular pub, except there had been a similar attack in Grantham on the same day. The other was less serious as the victim's two friends had intervened, but the attacker had escaped in a stolen van. It had been found, burnt out, three hours later in Wisbech. Three cars had been reported stolen in that area. They were being sought, but CCTV was intermittent in that part of

Cambridgeshire so the constabulary there was not hopeful of an imminent arrest.

    Ben's first thought was to warn Chris as he and Long John were living not too far away. Next he contacted Nick to see if he could provide some muscle to help protect them in Norfolk. He would pay top whack. Nick was happy to oblige and was sending up two of his best men.

Chapter 25

Parker had decided that he would deal with Knatchbull personally in order to identify the Enforcer, so they were at a loose end. They'd set out early to visit Chris and his homeless project. Going north, they'd had no trouble with the early morning sun. They'd alerted Chris that they'd be there for breakfast, a meal that all the colleagues ate together. Although the main house was still not finished, it was now weatherproof and the kitchen and dining room had been priorities for completion. Ben was certain they would live up to expectations as it seemed that Chris had become an excellent Clerk of the Works.

The welcome from Chris and Long John had been effusive and Chris had pointed out Nick's two heavies who were chatting happily with the other residents while enjoying an excellent full English. 'They've settled in well. They're both ex-army and they're certainly being good role models for our people. Can we keep them?'

Ben laughed. 'You'll have to talk to Nick Winter about that but I have a feeling that he might be keen to help you. He's one of that man's army who's made good.'

Long John touched the side of his nose and winked. 'The secret army, the one I mustn't mention. Mum's the word.' Then he left them to to join the group at the large circular table in the centre of the room.

After they'd collected their breakfasts at the serving hatch, 'Wow,' said Mary. 'This is what I'd expect from a good hotel. The sourdough is wonderful. I've given up making it, mine's always a bit yeasty. Where does it come from?'

'Local baker – we were planning to make our own in due course but have decided to support local businesses as best we can. We've had to go further for a butcher but we've found a good one. We'll try to grow our own veg and keep some chickens though.'

Ben replied, 'Get some guinea fowl. They make excellent

burglar alarms – and produce eggs that are wonderful for cakes.'

Chris laughed. 'How do you know that? But seriously, we're on it with the alarms.' He looked around in case there was anyone in earshot. 'Between you and me, I'm worried about the break-in. I could see what the local plods couldn't. There was obvious stuff that your average burglar would want and they didn't touch any of that. This was a high level job, the sort of thing that I'd have been doing in the past. I'm paranoid about privacy so we don't keep any personnel files on the computers here. That does mean that, if it was targeted at the charity, our colleagues files are safe. And that's a great relief. But I can't see who could be targeting us and why.'

Mary looked concerned. 'Have they got any further with your hit and run?'

'No. We're a bit backwoods here so I think they've shelved it. They picked up some local joyriders who were caught on CCTV shoplifting at the precise time we were run over so that came to nothing. That's gone quiet.'

Ben said, 'It could be coincidence but I don't like coincidences. OK. Let's see how you could have moved into the frame for targeting. Where have you been that you might have ruffled feathers?'

'Nowhere. We've been keeping local mostly, using local builders, architects, suppliers. We pay our bills regularly and are on good terms with everyone. A few nimbies were off at first but we've included them in the planning and they've all come on-side. The publican thinks it will enhance trade and we've made sure she knows that we'll deal with any problems. The local grandee is ex-navy and thinks this is a great idea. He's commended us on our plans for ensuring the residents are having a productive life. We have a No alcohol, No drugs policy on site and, with the help of the local doctors, we're keeping on top of that. And look around, the men all look happy and engaged.'

'What about further afield?'

'Only trip we've done is to see those army bigwigs and they were effusive in their response. They're all on board. Harris has done a grand job in corralling them into action and Long John was amazing. He really got them hooked. We're going to meet navy and airforce types next month. Long John says he'd like to do those too, even though the three services are different.'

'Sounds good. How many high-ups did you present to?'

'Twenty or so. Then we had lunch with them all. Long John was in his element. He's certainly found his calling.'

* * *

As Mary drove back, Ben was silent beside her. Without taking her eyes off the road, she asked. 'Are you thinking what I'm thinking?'

He smiled. 'You tell me what you're thinking and I'll say "Yes"'

'Long John.'

'Yes.'

'I haven't said what about him yet.'

'Tell me what about him then and I'll say "Yes" again.'

'When he was talking to us, he told us Chris's secret. I think that perhaps he might have said the wrong thing at the wrong time when he'd met the army high-ups. Spilled the secret army beans to the wrong person. This may be the break we're looking for.'

'Yes.'

'Is that all you can say?'

'No. Before we left, I had a word with Chris and I've phoned John Harris for a list of those who attended the briefing, with details of their regiments. I'm hoping we've interpreted Knatchbull's clues correctly. And I'm just hoping there aren't many Grenadiers who go sailing. If it were just the one, that would be handy. They're sending the photos immediately to Knatchbull. He should be able to identify one of them and then we can get him.'

'So, if Long John was loose tongued, it could be that his "careless words" will have found us our Enforcer. That puts him and Chris in the firing line.'

'I've warned Chris to be extra vigilant and not to let Long John out of his sight and I'll alert Parker and get him to add re-inforcements to Nick's two minders.' He dug his burner phone out of his pocket and relayed the news to Parker. When he came off the phone, his face was grave. He had more bad news to report. 'Glasgow One has attacked Knatchbull. He's in intensive care. They've put him in an induced coma. It's touch and go. I told them to play opera arias to him.'

'Oh, the poor man. Just as he seemed to be turning a corner.'

'Poor us too. He was our short-cut. How are we going to pin down the Enforcer without him?'

Chapter 26

'Do we know why?'

'No-one knows. G One isn't saying anything and Knatchbull can't. We just have to await events. I assume he broke through Knatchbull's cover. You ready for coffee?'

Ben sauntered out returning in a rush just a minute later. 'Ingleby's had a break-in.'

Mary was drying her hair. She turned off the dryer. 'He's the frightened one, isn't he? The one who cringed in the corner when he came to view Hutchinson?'

'Yes. Of all of them that I've met, he's one of the conspirators whose survival I'd most like to protect – him and Asquith. The burglary was at his home but he's been staying near his workplace in Holborn so it was his cleaner who noticed that his home computer was open when she'd last seen it closed. She thinks she saw someone running away but says it might just have been a jogger. Apparently, Ingleby has a serviced flat in Chancery Lane and MI5 thought he'd be safer there than at his house in Elstree.'

'Hold on,' said Mary. 'The rhyme says "one got in Chancery" so I'm not sure I'd have him staying there.'

'That's what I told Parker. But I'm afraid they're using him as bait. Not Parker's decision – it went to ministerial level and they over-ruled him. He's fuming. Have you heard anything from Sergei yet? I know communication with Ukraine isn't what it was, but it must have got to him by now.'

'Not a word. Henry assured me that it would get to him so I'll just wait and see what happens. Want anything from town? I've got to go and get some more wool. So annoying. It might not be the same batch.'

* * *

'Should I be worried? I got the wool and, as I was crossing Parker's Piece, I was sure I was being followed. The open space is a good place to see if anyone's tailing you and I'm certain that two young men in hoodies followed me home.'

Ben's heart missed a beat. 'I'll check with Parker.'

When Ben came off the phone, he shook his head. 'They're not MI5. Can you describe these two?'

'Young, looked as though they worked out, walked with ease. Their faces were hidden but I'd suspect late twenties. The main thing I noticed was that they walked with confidence. They probably saw me as an easy target for a mugging.'

'Yeah, be careful, eh? You're very precious to me. Do you want a minder?'

'No, I'll be careful – and remember, I have had self-defence training and I've got a gun. Just let them try anything!'

Ben looked sceptical. 'You're sure?'

Mary nodded so Ben replied, 'OK, I'll have to settle for that. But be very careful. Yes?' Mary nodded in a way that Ben could only construe as mock humility. He continued, 'Anyway, while you were out, Harris emailed me the list of army officers that Chris and Long John met. I phoned him and asked if it was complete and yes, that's the full list. I also asked if he'd seen Long John talking to anyone in particular. He laughed and said "Show me someone he didn't talk to". Apparently he was in full marketing mode. Harris was impressed and he said the others were too.'

Ben brought the list up on screen. 'I do so hope I interpreted Knatchbull's wrong tie as a clue. We've got five Grenadiers. Harris doesn't know if any of them sail. He says try Wiki.'

Mary was already on her computer looking up the five.

* * *

The three of them were sitting in Henry's study. They'd asked Katy to join them but she was engaged in a maths project which was 'frying her brain' so she'd declined. Secretly, Ben had been pleased. This was getting dangerous and her liaison with Chris meant that she was already a secondary target. He'd talked his feelings over with Alison Clare and they'd agreed that this was normal parental worry and was not a symptom of his PTSD. He and Alison had also agreed that, although there was no cure, his symptoms could continue to be managed in such a way that they disappeared. He hadn't had 'the dream' since Mary had entered his life. She was talking now and he looked across at her and smiled as he decided that he must be living under a very lucky star.

He laid out the photos for Henry to see. 'We've got five Grenadier officers, all Generals, all very high up and all the right age to have been in Ulster during "the troubles". Records show that they'd all had at least one NI posting. We've got a few avenues to follow. We've asked Allie and Ginny Murdock if they recognise any of the five as being friends with their father and we've drawn a blank there. They say Stanley Murdock kept all his contacts strictly separate from the family so they had no idea what he was doing.'

Henry shrugged. 'Well, at least he didn't involve them in his nefarious deeds.'

'But he did, the once. Remember, he took Allie on his visit to that Jacko – the paedophile terrorist. That was probably the last time he involved any of them.'

Henry grimaced. 'Good Lord, I'd forgotten that.'

Ben continued, 'Parker's dug up these photos of all five as they were in the nineties. It's twenty years ago and they all look similar with their army hair cuts. We'll ask the remaining conspirators too – but we can't rely on them to be truthful. Most of them seem to be convinced that it's the IRA or an offshoot that is targeting them so they think the Enforcer will be their protector. If they think that, they're not going to expose him. Asquith and Ingleby are our best bets so we'll see them first. Ingleby's next on the soldier boy list so he's a priority.'

Henry dabbed his eyes and passed a hand-written list to Ben. 'I wish I could help you more. But I have been digging with my old pals and I've come up with your five Generals in the order that they think the most likely, considering their lineage and the views they've espoused in the past. Army types are often cagey. Sometimes you'd think they were in my profession, keeping their cards so close to their barrel chests.'

Ben was puzzled. 'How do your spook friends know anything about these men? They're supposed to be pillars of the community, keeping us safe in our beds?'

Henry tapped the side of his nose. 'Ben! You were in

Military Intelligence. You know how it works. You kept files, yes?'

'Of course, but that was solely for Army use and kept inside our boundaries. We didn't share them with your lot.'

'And that's the crux. We had to have our own system. And I bet it was more thorough than yours! You'd be surprised the people we have files on. We're not like the Soviets, of course, but we just don't want to caught out when and if we need to watch or lean on people. The crying shame is that Murdock's lot slipped completely under our radar. It's caused more than a little angst to those parts of the service that know about it, I can tell you.'

Mary joined in. 'And secrecy being your middle name, you only tell those who need to know, on a "need to know" basis.'

'Precisely, and, if I'd gone in through the front door, I'd have been told I didn't need to know. I'd have had to go through Parker and you've seen how his grey men react to any sharing of intelligence. The bureaucracy would have taken weeks.'

'Thanks, Henry. Just keep those back channels open, will you? Anything more on the surviving conspirators?'

'Well, you know that Overton had his death notice published and is in a safe house until this is all over. Ingleby's a walking wreck, they say. My lot have him under close surveillance and I hear he's cracking under the strain. Seems that he and Asquith weren't true believers but once they were involved, they found they couldn't get out. The other two, Andrews and Thornhill, made a mint out of Northern Ireland and, we've no doubt, some of that came from Murdock's influence. Can't prove it but there's dirty money in there somewhere.'

'So we show our pictures of the five generals to Ingleby and Asquith and hope we get a positive ID. It means another trip to London and then to Devon.'

Mary looked at her diary. 'I don't think we can we fit either of them in before we meet the generals.' She turned to Henry. 'Harris has set up a meeting tomorrow with the five Grenadier Generals. He's told them that we are trustees of Chris's charity and we'd like to thank them. He's fabricated a few stats to show that Grenadiers are more likely to succumb to PTSD and other mental illnesses so their help will be vital. We'd rather have left it till we'd known more, but needs must and Harris has been a boon to the charity.'

Henry patted Ben's arm. 'You know, old boy, it would help if you wore your medals.'

'Harris said that. I've dug them out and Mary's made sure they're clean and shiny. But I feel such a fraud. They're undeserved. I didn't know what I was doing.'

Mary squeezed Ben's arm and spoke to Henry. 'He's got imposter syndrome so needed to be sure it would make a difference.'

Henry looked straight at Ben. 'Utter drivel and nonsense. They don't give the VC to every Tom, Dick or Harry. At the very least, one of them will know who you are and what you did. They'd be scandalised if you aren't wearing all your gongs. They'll have theirs paraded across their chests. They'll be exceedingly jealous of yours, of course, but they probably won't show it.'

'It was good of Harris to set this up but I'm not sure what we'll get out of it.'

Henry looked glum. 'Mmm, a bit tricky. You realise that, if Chris and Long John are being targeted, you'll be putting yourselves in the same firing line.'

Ben replied, 'Needs must. We've got to get this stopped and we're moving far too slowly. If this brings the Enforcer out into the open, then he can be dealt with.'

'Don't forget, he's a highly trained killer and he's got another highly trained killer working for him.'

'We won't.'

* * *

They were seated very comfortably in a private room beside the Officers Mess. The journey to Wellington Barracks had been uneventful and it was obvious, on arrival, that they were going to get the full treatment as important guests. The brief tour of the Officers' Mess and other impressive rooms had been conducted by a sergeant who had been officious until Ben had removed his coat and revealed the string of medals across his chest. Ben had almost laughed out loud as the term 'his eyes nearly popped out of his head' became a reality. The sergeant's demeanour had swivelled

180 degrees at the sight of Ben's Victoria Cross. Mary, who they had previously decided would be silent and subservient so she could observe from the background, had nearly blown her cover but had managed to avoid Ben's eyes and stifle her giggles.

They were being served coffee and twiddly biscuits. It brought to Ben's mind the biscuit that he had nearly choked on when he had first met Stanley Murdock's killer. Josephine Finlay, by letting Murdock die, had inadvertently started the process that had brought this cabal of conspirators into the open. Without her, elements of this grouping would have skulked in the background waiting for the opportunity to foment division and wreak havoc in Northern Ireland. Britain had a lot to thank Josephine Finlay for, and they would never know the debt they owed her. She and her mother were now happily settled in Hunstanton with Ben's Uncle Mo an almost permanent guest. Ben knew that a visit to them was long overdue. When this was over they would have to take a trip to the seaside.

Ben's reverie was broken by the arrival of the five generals, all in full regalia. They all, in turn, pumped Ben's hand, taking full account of his medals. Ben and Mary could now put faces to the names they had on their list from Harris. The five had obviously been well briefed as one of them turned to Mary and said, 'Amelina, such an interesting surname. Russian, is it?'

Mary's demure look would have put a princess to shame. 'I was briefly married to a Russian. It was over long ago but I like having a name at the beginning of the alphabet so I've kept his name and nothing else. I'm soon to be married to Ben so then I'll be Mary Burton.'

Her uncertain smile as she dropped her gaze completed the act. The general who had asked her, now confirmed as General Sir Walter Craig, patted her hand and agreed, 'Glad you'll be staying at the start of the alphabet – it has its advantages. Oh, and congratulations on your impending nuptials.'

General Craig took the lead and formally introduced them to the other four. 'My esteemed colleagues.' He smiled, 'In strict alphabetical order, General Sir George Crowther-Leakey, General John Sadler, General Abraham Stern and General Charles Wells. And, can I say, on behalf of all of us here, how delighted we are to have such a distinguished former soldier on board for this project in Norfolk.'

Ben smiled at them all while trying to gauge their response – knowing that Mary would be doing a much better job of this analysis than he. She would be on the alert throughout for any 'tells' or other signs of discomfort or understanding outside the norm. He thought back to his time in the army. At that time, it hadn't occurred to him how unequal the military world had been, and looking round at these five eminent military men it seemed to be still the case. This place was opulent; it reminded him of any officers mess but this one was on steroids. With his medals paraded, he was considered the star while Mary was patronised. He knew this was the effect they had wanted, but it still made him feel uncomfortable.

They sat and talked around the project for nearly an hour with Ben pushing, as he thought appropriate for a Trustee, for further funding and involvement. Making sure Mary had full view of the five, he waited till their discussion had nearly reached its conclusion before mentioning Long John. 'I gather you've all met Long John? I first met him when he was living rough in Norfolk. Such a transformation. He's a good exemplar for this project.'

There were enthusiastic nods and agreement that he was an asset to the project. Ben waited for a verbal response. Craig complied. 'Yes, he certainly is a great asset. He got us all fired up.'

After another brief pause, Ben filled the silence with their their pre-arranged statement – a statement based on a lie. 'On a totally different matter, and quite separate from this project, I recently conducted the funeral of Sir James Hutchinson.' For Mary's benefit, he paused for a few seconds before continuing. 'One of the mourners, Sir John Sheringham was, I believe, a former Grenadier. He has recently been killed in a motor-cycle accident. My commiserations.'

Craig looked around the other four. 'Sheringham? Anyone know a Sheringham?' As they all shook their heads, he turned to Ben, 'You've caught us unawares there. We'll have to follow up on that. Thank you for bringing it to our attention.'

* * *

They'd settled in a quiet corner at the back of The Buckingham Arms. In the short walk from the barracks, they had been silent by mutual consent, each wanting to put their thoughts in order. Ben took a long drink of his beer and sighed appreciatively. 'Good stuff. Now, Mary, my eyes and ears, my demure and obsequious little woman, tell me what you know.'

Mary gave him one of her 'looks'. He interpreted it as saying, I love you, you sarky bugger. Out loud she replied, 'I'll just keep you in suspense. First, the call from Parker just now. Any news?'

'Knatchbull, no change. They put him in an induced coma and he hasn't stabilised yet so it could be a long haul – or worse. You know, even though he tried to kill us, I've grown quite fond of him. I enjoy our chats, and that's beside the thrill of deciphering the little clues he keeps giving us. He was consumed with hate for his cousin's killers but I think he's come to terms with that and has realised how deranged his actions were. I hope he survives and they let him out. I don't think he'll be a danger to anyone now. He wants to become a Quaker and go to the opera. I hope he gets the chance.'

He took a long draught of his beer then continued, 'Now his attacker – that's another kettle of fish altogether. His attacker is silent on all fronts. He's a real hard nut. I don't think they'll get anything out of him. And you heard me remonstrating with Parker about using Ingleby as bait, but they're not budging. The powers that be, they think it's a risk worth taking – one guilty life as opposed to many innocents. Parker says they have Ingleby well covered and it's their best chance of catching the Enforcer or the other Glasgow killer, but it doesn't feel right to me. They've lied to him, telling him he's safer in London. We've been put on the front line in the past, but we always knew the odds. Ingleby doesn't.'

Mary replied, 'It's a murky world. We've always known that. In the distant past, we were in deep, but now, it's a world we want to stay on the periphery of. Down to business. I wouldn't tell you any of our Generals' history before you met them so you could have an open mind.'

'Yes, so you can tell me now.'

'Not so fast. I want to know your impressions first.'

Ben sighed. 'Confused! I didn't get much. The only one I warmed to was Wells. He seemed the most open and was the most enthusiastic about the project. I wouldn't like him to be the Enforcer. The rest seemed to be holding back but I suppose they're dyed in the wool army types so, what can we expect?'

Mary smiled. 'Well, your luck's in. Wells comes from an old Catholic family who even have a Catholic martyr as an ancestor. Saint Swithun Wells was hanged in Elizabeth's reign. Our man no longer goes to mass but his wife and four sons are regular communicants at Westminster Cathedral. I hardly think he'd be part of a cabal to exterminate Catholics. And, remember, the Enforcer was chosen by Stanley Murdock, who was a very clever strategist. He wouldn't choose a Catholic – even a lapsed one. So, I think Wells is the only one that we can rule out completely.'

'Oh good. I really liked him. So Craig, Crowther-Leakey, Sadler and Stern, what of them?'

Mary replied, 'They've all been fun to research and what it shows me is that power stays within a small cabal. Illustrious ancestors one and all. I'm going first for the person I think least likely to be the one to be our prime suspect. OK?' Ben nodded, so Mary continued, 'Let's start with Stern. He also has a famous ancestor.'

Ben interrupted, 'Not Avraham Stern!'

'The very same, the leader of the Stern Gang. General Stern has extensive family in Israel and, if this were a plot to kill Palestinians, he would be our prime suspect.'

Ben was thoughtful. 'There are parallels though, between Israel and Ireland. The Israelis were put into a land already occupied by Palestinians; likewise the Protestant settlers in Ulster and before that, the imposition of English landlords throughout Ireland. They were placed there to contain the Catholics. Could he have transferred antipathy to the Palestinians and placed it on Catholics?'

Mary looked sceptical. 'It has legs, but not if he's following family tradition. The Stern Gang were fighting a colonial power – that's us, not the Palestinians. But he might have moved on. The two sides in the Middle East have been at each other's throats since Balfour ballsed it up. As had the Protestants and Catholics before the Good Friday Agreement. We can't rule out that he's made some sort of transference of hostility from the Palestinian population to the Catholic one.'

'We need to keep him in the frame then, but what about his demeanour?'

'His non-verbal signals were all positive. He didn't bat an eyelid when you mentioned Hutchinson's or Sheringham's deaths, so he's a doubtful.'

'Good. Who's next?'

'Sadler. He's the direct descendent of Michael Thomas Sadler who was briefly MP for Newark in the early eighteen hundreds. He was against Catholic emancipation but he did want to upgrade the agriculture there. Way before the famine, he saw the problem with monoculture and wanted to diversify farming practice in Ireland. He was prescient in foretelling that the reliance on one crop would lead to disaster if this crop should fail. He retired to Belfast and died there.'

Mary looked down at the paper in her hand. 'Ah, here it is. He wanted the introduction of legal provision for the poor and needy, discouragement of absentee landlords and encouragement of their residence on their property in Ireland and, because Ireland was essentially an agricultural country, the introduction of an efficient Corn Law.'

'So, Sadler's ancestor was progressive even though he didn't agree with Irish emancipation. Can we assume his descendants are too?'

'No, but I've done further ferreting into the present General Sadler. He's is a communicant member of the Church of England and a patron of several charities including one for farmers facing mental issues.'

'So the agrarian theme continues.'

'He's a large land-owner in Scotland – cattle and arable plus vast expanses of moorland for shooting, if that means anything.'

'No idea. Did he seem to recognise the names of our plotters?'

Mary shook her head. 'No discernable reaction.'

'Next?'

'Crowther-Leakey. The Crowthers were more humble but

were a Protestant family in Dublin. They lost their power with Catholic Emancipation so the family became instrumental in setting up the Dublin Orange Lodge. Then they moved to America and had rows with Catholic neighbours there. After that, it all cooled down and they settled in as Americans. One came back and married a Leakey. The Leakey's are mostly artists and fossil hunters but a number have been decorated soldiers. They're spread between Somerset and Kenya.

'Mau-mau?'

'Yep, one killed in the uprising.'

'Religious affiliation now?'

'C of E but none of the family seems to go to church.'

Ben looked puzzled. 'So why is he higher up the list than Sadler and Stern?'

'He reacted to Hutchinson's name.'

'Ah!'

'When you said you'd recently buried Sir James Hutchinson and you thought Sheringham had some ties with the Grenadiers, he sort of jumped – looked startled. We know it's a complete fabrication that there's any Grenadier connection but there was definitely a reaction from Crowther-Leakey. He knew Hutchinson, definitely. And and possibly Sheringham too.'

'And Craig, why is he top of the list?'

'Craig's from the Craigavon family, consequently his background makes him favourite for our Enforcer. The first Viscount Craigavon was a Unionist MP who armed Protestant paramilitaries in the early nineteen hundreds. He was violently opposed to Irish independence and instrumental in making sure that there were six not nine counties in Northern Ireland so the Protestant vote would continue to outnumber the Catholic in that part of Ireland. He was the first Prime minister of Northern Ireland.

'General Craig's mother is a descendant of that family. A scandal at the time was that she wasn't married to his father and wouldn't say who the father was. Unless General Craig knows, then the secret has gone with her to her grave. Hence his name is Craig through his mother's side.'

'It would have been a huge scandal. You couldn't find out any more?'

'No. They were very good at hushing it up. In this case, money refused to talk.'

'And now?'

'No religious affiliation. Nothing to link him with Protestant extremism. Like the rest of them, an unblemished record. He did know Sheringham though. He raised his eyebrows at the link with the Grenadiers. Then, when you mentioned Sheringham being at Hutchinson's funeral, his brows drew together and he turned away, ostensibly to blow his nose. So I think he knew both of them – and if he knew both, it's possible, even probable, that he knows the others. What do you think?'

'Did you see Crowther-Leakey react to the mention of Sheringham?'

'That's the annoying bit. As Craig turned, he got in my line of sight. Crowther-Leakey was behind him so I couldn't see him. Could you?'

'Um, he reacted but it might have been to Craig's nose-blowing. Loud, wasn't it. I think our General Craig could double as a foghorn on the Thames on a misty night. They all jumped so I'm none too sure who knows what.'

Chapter 27

The phone rang at 5.40 a.m. As Ben rose from a deep and dreamless sleep, he could hear Mary shouting into the receiver. She was using words he'd never heard her use before. He vowed then that he would never get on the wrong side of her – it would be a terrifying experience.

She stomped back into the bedroom with tears streaming down her cheeks. He was immediately gripped by a knot of fear. 'What is it?'

'Ingleby. He's dead. They let the bastards get to him. You warned them that the rhyme said he'd die "in Chancery" and they took diddly-squat notice. The fucking bastards. He was one of the repentant ones. He shouldn't have died. They should have protected him.' She took a shuddering breath and Ben held her. He decided to keep quiet until he was certain she had vented all her anger, but he found himself letting out a sigh of relief that this did not concern anyone closer to home. She continued, 'They lied to him; said he'd be safe. And those bastards managed to get to him.'

Ben hugged her to him. She relaxed for a moment then pulled away. 'And do you know what the worst of it is?'

Ben said quietly, 'Tell me.'

'My very first thought was that we wouldn't be able to show him the pictures of the Generals. Am I turning into a monster, Ben? Am I turning into one of them?'

He gently stroked her hair. 'No, my love. Look at you. You're feeling the injustice of it all; the injustice that they let Ingleby die, the injustice that it's a setback that keeps us from getting to the real monsters, the injustice that it may be that other innocents will die while we're trying to close in on those killers.'

Mary smiled a tremulous smile. 'I love you, Ben Burton. Never forget that.'

'Cup of tea time. We can make an early start.'

As they drank tea in the kitchen, they considered the possibility that their visit to the Generals had precipitated Ingleby's death and came to the sorry conclusion that it could be so. Mary explained the manner of his death; asphyxiation. 'He was found at about three this morning on the routine surveillance round. Parker says the operative who found him is now in intensive care. They think a nerve agent was used and they've had to evacuate the building and put a cordon round it.'

The phone rang again, and this time Ben answered it. He listened intently and nodded and grunted several times. 'Yes, she's fine. Yes, we need to move fast. And yes, we'll do what we can.' He tapped to end the call and put the phone down. He ran his fingers through his hair. 'That was Parker. Ingleby was murdered using a nerve agent called VX. It's stored at Porton Down. They have no idea how some of it came to leave the base. They've got men in hazard suits cleaning Ingleby's place but, so far, it seems to have been restricted to the handle to flush the loo.'

Mary typed VX on her tablet. 'They must be getting desperate. Good God! It's considered a weapon of mass destruction. Says here it would be less volatile if it were in a solid. So that's presumably why they chose the loo flush, less likely to spread than if it were in an aerosol or liquid form. Did they say how they think it got there?'

'No break-in but he had a visitor yesterday evening. He was checked in by the security man on duty. He showed a driving licence in the name of Peter Andrews. The guard checked with DVLA and it all seemed in order. Ingleby confirmed that he was an old friend so they let him in.'

'They're bringing in Andrews now. He's a rich bigwig so it's a bit tricky!'

'Any description of the man – I don't suppose there's CCTV? Did he have a Glaswegian accent?'

'He spoke impeccable Received English. Cut glass, the guard said. He was tall and upright with, and I quote, "military bearing". The CCTV is being looked at but the guard's description could have fitted Andrews or any of our generals.'

'We think Andrews continued to be a true believer so, if it was him, either he was coerced or he was misled or, more chilling, he was willing to be a party to this murder. If the latter, he won't be any use. He won't believe he's next on the list.'

* * *

At six a.m. they were on the road, driving to London to meet Parker for an interview with Andrews. Mary was driving. She had often told Ben that she was the better driver and the worse passenger. Each time she'd said this, he'd questioned the former and agreed with the latter. Ben's burner from Parker started its insistent ring. The phonecall took a long time with Ben saying little but grunting at intervals. When he came off the phone, he said, 'Might as well slow down. They searched for Andrews in his London flat. The concierge said he hadn't been there all week but a friend had stopped by and asked him to deliver a note to Andrews. The concierge had left it on the kitchen worktop in Andrews' flat. On opening it, the operatives found it was a suicide note saying he had gone to his boat to kill himself. He wasn't in his flat so they sent a team down to his boat. Good job they went with full hazard gear. He was wearing rubber gloves but dead as a dodo. They found a miniscule amount of VX solidified with clay. Further investigation showed that he had two pairs of nitrile gloves, both contaminated with the nerve gas. The ones he was wearing had pinprick holes in the finger tips. They surmise that he was told to wear the first pair at Ingleby's flat and the second when he was disposing of the evidence. Of course, this makes it a double murder.'

'But why plant the suicide note? Surely that was a dangerous move. It brought the Enforcer out into the open.'

'He wore a scarf round his face and dark glasses. The concierge said he wouldn't know him again.'

They were silent for a while then Mary banged on the steering wheel. 'Of course! It was to keep to the rhyme. There has to be a red herring for Andrews' death. *"Four little Soldier Boys going out to sea; a red herring swallowed one and then there were three."* I think the note was our red herring. We know Murdock was mad, bad and extremely dangerous. Seems it was infectious! We are dealing with another seriously unhinged person.'

'And we are doing a seriously shit job of protecting his victims.'

Chapter 28

'Are you sure you'll be OK?'

'Mary, you're only going to be gone for two nights. We're at a stand-still with the murders and now Asquith has said he can't identify the army type at that meeting we've got to have a rethink. Anyway, you could do with a break. Of course I'll be OK. Have a great time and give my love to Mo and Josephine and Agnes. Tell them, if I hadn't had to help Michael with this funeral, I'd have been up there with you breathing in the salt air and gobbling fish and chips.'

'I'll phone, once I've settled in. We're going to have a quiet day today and I'm really looking forward to Josephine's pamper day tomorrow. It's at some posh hotel nearby. The thought of that massage is giving me goosebumps.'

Ben gave her a last hug and waved goodbye. When Josephine had suggested that they should come to visit, they'd been delighted to accept. Then, this big and important funeral had come up. He'd discussed with Alison Clare the idea of Mary going alone and they'd agreed that it was a good idea and could be used as a test. Mary had not left his side since their trips to Ireland searching for 'Kevin's cousin'. They'd found Tommy and with him the tale of Murdock's treachery had begun to unfold. They'd also found each other and they were a good team – there was no doubting that. Since joining forces with Mary, his PTSD had abated. For the first time in nearly twenty years, he was reacting normally to the vicissitudes of life. And now, the test. Could he, left alone in the house without Mary, without Mo, without his two daughters, keep his demons at bay? Alison thought he could and so did he. Today, he would be helping Michael and Pam with the big funeral.

* * *

The day done and the funeral over, Ben sat down with his Indian takeaway to watch some rubbish on television. Mary hadn't phoned and he'd decided not to call her. In the hurly burly of seeing Josephine and family, he was sure she had forgotten. If she hadn't got in touch by the morning, he'd decide then whether to call her. It was with some pride that he'd found that he'd been able to give her some space.

Revelling in the peace of being alone, he realised that, in nearly twenty years living there, this was the first time that he had spent the night alone in this house. There had always been Katy and Sarah to look after, and Katy had only moved out when Mary had moved in. He breathed a happy sigh then shook himself. This was no time for relaxation; he needed to think.

They had a job and it was not going well. Out of their list of conspirators, two had been killed before the Services had become aware of the murders, one was in hiding, four more had been killed despite all their efforts to keep them alive and only two were still living. The last one of these, Asquith, had shown real regret for his part and had been as helpful as he could be, but still had not been able to identify the Enforcer. It seemed that the man in the army uniform had only attended the one meeting and had stood at the back. That meeting was the one that Murdock had secretly filmed in order to to acquire evidence against them all. And yet, the Enforcer's face had not been shown on that video, nor were there any distinguishing features to the uniform.

Ben sat up suddenly. His brain was fizzing, posing the question they had so far omitted to ask themselves. Why? Why was this one man still incognito? If Murdock had wanted evidence to guarantee obedience, why had he allowed the army man to remain in the shadows? And why had this man not been mentioned in any of Murdock's stash of evidence? Into Ben's mind came a truly unwelcome and thoroughly horrifying thought. They had always believed that Stanley Murdock had been the prime mover and he was dead. They had believed that Knatchbull had been the second-in-command and he was incarcerated. They had assumed that the leaders were incapacitated. But, what if it had not been Murdock in charge of the genocidal plan? What if it had been the Enforcer who had been the prime mover with Murdock merely his Chief-of-Staff? That would explain his keeping to the rhyme even after Murdock's death. If it were the Enforcer's rhyme and not Murdock's, the

Enforcer would be more likely to be wedded to it. If this hypothesis were true, then they could be dealing with someone even more dangerous than Stanley Murdock.

Since their visit to the Generals, they had discounted the three remaining conspirators as the Enforcer. The evidence was circumstantial, but all three had been under surveillance when the murders of their compatriots had been committed. Overton was was under lock and key, and, of the remaining two at large, Thornhill and Asquith, Lord Thornhill seemed to be the only 'true believer' and Parker's people had kept him under close scrutiny. His communications had been monitored and they were sure that he was innocent of these murders. So it came back to the Generals.

Ben wished Mary were here to act as his sounding board. If she hadn't phoned by the morning, he would call to ask her. In the meantime he would phone Parker to share these unwelcome thoughts. After that phone call, Ben went back to the list of conspirators. It was displayed on the fridge together with the rhyme. Ben read the last bit aloud.

'Three little Soldier Boys walking in the zoo; A big bear hugged one and then there were two.
Two little Soldier Boys sitting in the sun; One got frizzled up and then there was one.
One little Soldier Boy left all alone; He went out and hanged himself and then there were none.'

The Enforcer was a conundrum as was the one little soldier boy. Were they one and the same? Ben came to the conclusion that they could be – but that was not a given. As he mulled this over, his phone burst into life. It was Josephine. She asked when was Mary arriving and why wasn't she answering her phone?

* * *

Three hours later Ben had contacted all the hospitals between Cambridge and Hunstanton. No-one of Mary's description had been admitted. He'd contacted Parker to get his help and his people had quickly swung into action. He'd told Parker that Mary had thought she was being followed. Their initial enquiries suggested that Mary had disappeared into thin air. Then her car was found abandoned near Bishops Stortford with her phone lodged in the glove compartment. That was all they had. She'd gone in the opposite direction to the one in which she was supposed to travel and had disappeared.

Ben knew he needed to keep busy in order to prevent his brain going into overdrive in surmising what could have happened. Parker had alerted all the authorities. They were doing the overdrive bit on his behalf so it was out of his hands. Every time his brain took him to thinking of life without Mary he brought it swiftly back to the present. As time wore on, it was becoming more and more difficult to keep his brain on track. It was now five hours since Josephine's phone call. Ben looked at his watch, eleven pm. He repeated all the exercises that Alison Clare had given him. So far, he'd kept himself together but he needed something more.

He hadn't yet contacted Henry, Mary's oldest friend. He knew that Henry was not in the best of health and had not wanted to worry him. Even at this late hour, he would go to see him; to tell him in person that Mary was missing. As Henry hardly left the confines of Ethel's these days, Ben was certain he would be found in his rooms in college. He was right.

Henry greeted him with a hug. Even in his agitated state, Ben noticed that Henry's slippers were now in the last stages of decrepitude and he vowed to buy the old man a new pair when this was over. He quickly related the news of Mary's disappearance.

Henry's response was not at all as Ben had expected. He sat down heavily and sighed. 'Oh dear! The silly boy. I thought I'd dissuaded him. Bishops Stortford, you say? Several small airfields near there. They'd have taken off from one of those.'

'Henry, what are you talking about. Mary is missing. Did you take that in?'

'Oh yes, dear boy. And I know precisely where she is.'

'Is she safe?'

'As safe as anyone is in Crimea these days. We'd better get something in place to get her out. Phone Parker, will you. I'm assuming she won't have her passport with her. Tell him she's in Ukraine and we've got to extract her.'

Ben's very rudimentary knowledge of Russian meant that most of Henry's WhatsApp conversation with Sergei was gibberish to him. He recognised Лох as 'gullible idiot'. The rest of the stream of Henry's invective was lost on him. Ben gesticulated early in the phone call to ask if Mary was OK. Henry nodded and mouthed, 'Yes.' That was all Ben wanted to know. The explanation for her kidnap could come later. And now he knew that she was safe, all his previous fears could come to the surface. He consciously decided to acknowledge them, one by one, and then discard them as Dr Clare had advised. He did this as he waited impatiently for Henry to finish his call.

'Well?'

'Sergei says he is in immediate danger; he knows he's on a Kremlin watch list. He wanted to square things with Mary in case he's taken or killed. Such a stupid thing to do! At least he had the sense to meet her in a secret location near Lviv. It's over near the Polish border so well away from Crimea. Parker will probably get her into Poland and fly her from there.'

Ben sat down and put his head in his hands. The rush of relief hit him squarely in his chest and nearly knocked him backwards. He took several deep breaths before looking over at Henry. He handed Henry a clean handkerchief and said, 'Mop up your tears, old friend. She'll soon be on her way home.'

Henry wiped his eyes. 'I'm so sorry, Ben. He was always a bit of a hot-head. That's probably why he risked everything to marry Mary. He told me he had to see her to tell her in person why he'd left her all those years ago and why he'd never contacted her. I suggested he came to London or we'd organise that they meet in Poland. I said I'd help from this end and he should wait a few days. I thought that's what he would do. Then you said that Mary thought she was being followed and I started to worry.'

'So the two people following Mary were Sergei's men?'

Henry nodded. 'It seems so.'

'And they abducted her and took her to Ukraine and kept her out of contact. I'm beginning to dislike Sergei intensely!' Ben would have said more but Henry's phone interrupted him.

Henry answered and handed the phone to Ben. 'It's Mary.'

***

As Henry and Ben sat drinking g and t's far stronger than Mary would have allowed, Henry recounted the rest of his conversation with Sergei. 'He's in fear of his life, and more importantly to him, the lives of his family. He's moved them out of Russia and they're staying with his wife's family in Lviv. I offered to get them out so they could resettle here but Ludmilla won't countenance leaving Ukraine. He's certain that Putin is about to annex Crimea. That will be his next step in order to see what the Allies will do. Sergei has his agents to protect so he's trying to move them all to the west of Ukraine, but they're a bolshie lot and some say they'll stay to fight.' Henry stopped to wipe his eyes again. 'They're on a war footing and Sergei is preparing for the worst, so don't be too hard on him. He wanted to put his house in order in case of …'

Ben interrupted him. 'It's OK. Don't worry. I won't. Mary told me not to think badly of him. He did what he needed to do. When does he think the invasion will happen?'

'He says early next year. The winter's closing in so he reckons he's got till April next year to get his people out of danger, then obliterate all record of his network and lay some false trails. Then, if they'll have him, he'll join up and fight somewhere on the Eastern Front.'

'A brave man indeed and, to be honest, I'm indebted to him. No need to look so sceptical, Henry. I see this as a test. It's not one I would have imposed on myself but Mary was missing and I didn't fall apart. I continued to function. Yes, I was terrified. Yes, I kept thinking the worst, but I coped. That's what I call progress.'

Henry's response was typical. 'That calls for a celebration, my friend. Another g and t I think. While the cat's away in Ukraine etc.'

'While we celebrate our good fortune, we should also drink to Ukraine and freedom. What makes Sergei so certain that Putin will invade?'

'Georgia 2008. It's part of a pattern. As soon as there is a significant move to westernise in one of the old Soviet republics, Putin acts to stop it. He wants them all back, the greater Russia and all that. We keep pacifying him and we will do until we realise that he doesn't understand compromise. We need to wake up and learn that he only understands force. Anyway, nothing more we can do there. Our politicians are deaf to the warnings. Now we know Mary is safe, you can bring me up to date on our own little genocidal plot.'

'Settle yourself in, Henry. I have a theory I want to run past you. It's about the real leader of this cabal and it's not Murdock.'

Chapter 29

'We're going to have to do it again, aren't we? It's the only way to flush him out and now we believe he's ultra-dangerous, he's got to be stopped.'

Mary had been back home for just over an hour and they had already decided to put themselves in the line of fire in order to stop the Enforcer – or the leader as they now thought of him – from continuing his deadly rampage.

Mary had told Ben of her trip to Ukraine in a tiny plane and that despite her pleadings, her two captors had not let her phone Ben or even Henry. Her Russian was rusty but had been sufficient for her to understand that Sergei would decide. Ben's one question had been, 'Why didn't you use your gun?'

And she had replied, 'Their first words were, "Sergei sent us. We will not hurt you," so how could I?' She hadn't told Ben any details of her conversation with her former husband and he had decided that she would tell him in her own good time. It had been sufficient to know that she was home and safe.

They'd informed Henry that Mary was home. Henry was in his element, liaising with Sergei and Parker in order to try to keep Sergei's web of informants intact. If Putin were to invade Crimea, they would be a vital source of information and Henry was working hard to persuade them not to become cannon fodder. He had insisted to Sergei that they were far too important to the West for them to be wantonly killed.

Mary took another sip of her wine, savoured it, then asked in a non-committal voice, 'So how do we go about it? Same as Knatchbull? Tell them we have information that they wouldn't want to get into the public domain. What do you think? If we do that, we could use that deserted farm where we caught Knatchbull. The services are using it for training now so it will be available. '

Ben smiled. He'd got used to Mary's softly, softly approach, her way of persuading him to her way of thinking by asking his opinion. His smile was his admission to himself that, with him, it always worked. 'Could do. Worked last time. But last time we had army back-up. We'll have to talk to Parker about the logistics but I'm not sure we can rely on asking soldiers to shoot their own General, for that's what it might come to.'

'And we're not sure who in the army might be amenable to his cause or cajoled into helping him. So we'll probably be covered by the men in black, the same as when you made yourself a sitting duck for that paedophile.'

Ben smiled a rueful smile. 'It's getting to be habit forming, isn't it.'

* * *

Parker and his three grey men were looking down at their papers so Ben could not gauge their response. He decided to try again, more assertively. 'We'll need two or three marksmen strategically placed. Two can be hidden in the wall; the third in the false chimney. And further marksmen in those holes in the ground.'

Parker looked up. 'I will do the arrest.'

He might just as well have pulled puppet strings on his three associates. Their heads jerked up in unison. 'No! You can't,' said the first.

'It's far too dangerous,' said the second.

'It must be a field operative. You haven't been in the field for years.'

Parker looked straight at Ben. 'I want to be the person to take this man into custody.' Then he turned to Mary. 'What do you think?'

Mary smiled, 'You and Henry are trying to persuade Sergei not to go to the front line. The question for you is, are you more useful behind the lines?'

Parker sighed. 'Of course. Behind the lines, behind a desk. You've no idea how much I miss the buzz. But you're right. I'll be there, though I'll stay behind the lines. And, of course, there may be no arrest.'

He looked at his grey man. They all nodded agreement.

The logistics would be very similar to those employed in the arrest of Knatchbull. The plan was that they would send a message to all their suspects, Generals Craig, Crowther-Leakey, Sadler, Stern and Wells. Even Wells whose forebears included a Catholic martyr was not to be excluded. The message would contain detail that only the Enforcer would know. As before, the message would be sent at short notice so he would have little time to rally any troops and it would state that he should come alone. Again, it would take the form of an unsophisticated blackmail attempt by an extortionist.

Parker asked, 'Why do you think it has to be you? Why not one of my men posing as an unknown extortionist?'

'Because I've rattled their cage. I've put the thought in their mind that I know more than I should.'

Parker turned to the grey man on his left. 'Get in touch with Harris. I'm pretty sure the army top brass were kept in ignorance when he organised it last time. Make sure that's the case, will you?'

The grey man nodded. 'Noted.'

Parker turned to Ben. 'I'll let you know the outcome.'

Ben had not told Mary in advance that he would suggest he go it alone. He'd thought she would protest when he raised it, but yet again she surprised him.

'Yes, sensible. I'd be another target so that would split the hazard but I'd also be a distraction for the marksmen. On balance I think I'd be a liability.'

So it was decided. As it was near Christmas, they would set it in motion in early January. Then it was to be a repeat performance of the blackmail of Knatchbull but this time without Mary and without the army back-up. They would be keeping the army in ignorance.

Chapter 30

Ben and Mary had agreed that their Christmas with their family and friends in Norfolk with Chris and his band of ex-soldiers had been the best ever. They'd played stupid party games, they'd worn silly hats and they'd laughed until their sides had ached. They'd been to midnight mass even though neither believed, they'd had roast goose and too many trimmings, they'd watched the Queen's speech and had cried watching 'It's a wonderful life'. The only alcohol to have passed their lips had been when they had accompanied Henry to the pub so he could have his one and only g and t each evening. For Ben, there had been the tiny niggle at the back of his mind that this might be Henry's last or even his own last Christmas. He had managed to keep that niggle at bay.

Now, they were sitting comfortably with Henry in his study. The plan to smoke out the Enforcer was in full swing. Ben just had to wait to be called to action. The format was to be almost exactly that of the previous trap except this time neither Chris nor the army would be involved. Ben had been relieved when Parker had relayed the message that none of the targeted generals had been involved or informed of the action last time. So it had been concluded that the Enforcer would not know about Knatchbull's arrest and would believe him to be dead. His actions in carrying out the plan 'after the cake had been demolished' backed up this assertion. Harris had assured them that the marksmen involved in the capture of Knatchbull had not been informed of the identity of their target so he was as sure as he could be that there had been no leakage of vital information.

Mary sighed. 'That's as much as we can hope for, I suppose. MI5 will be sending a clip of the conspirators' meeting and telling them that they mustn't tell anyone and they must come alone, otherwise the information and their involvement in the plot will be forwarded to the appropriate authorities and the press.'

Henry nodded slowly. 'Not watertight but it seldom is. We take risks.'

Ben smiled at them both. 'I'm confident the men in black will cover me. They didn't let that paedophile doctor get near me. Correct me if I'm wrong, Henry, but I have the feeling that this one will be the same – they'll want to take no prisoners.'

Henry nodded. 'Could be. If he dies, they'll fabricate some story to explain his death. But I think they'll want to take this one alive. He has valuable information.'

Ben continued, 'I've agreed with Parker that I need to talk to the Enforcer; that his marksmen must hold their fire. We must get to the truth and try to find out if there is anyone involved that we still don't know about.'

Mary asked, 'So, Henry, who would you put your money on to turn up for this meet?'

'Well, my dear, it's not clear-cut, is it? But then, if it were, you wouldn't be doing it. Stern has Jewish heritage and Wells is of Catholic stock so I'd be very surprised if it were one of those two. Craig's Craigavon background makes him a prime candidate and you think he may have known two of the conspirators. Same for Crowther-Leakey. I'd bet on one or the other. But then, there's Sadler. They're all three firmly on the Protestant side of the religious divide. Pity we don't know who Craig's father was. That might have given us more to go on. Also a pity he restricted your view of Crowther-Leakey when Sheringham was mentioned. I think it could be any of those three. Have we got anything else to go on?'

'No. Parker's done some more digging but hasn't come up with anything useful. Nothing to differentiate between the three.'

Henry asked, 'What about military intelligence? They'll need to be informed and they might have something to add.'

Ben answered. 'That could have been a tricky one, treading on military toes etc, but it seems Parker has an old friend there who he's liaising with. He's making sure that it remains his operation but that military intelligence know enough about what's going on to feel included but will keep their distance. They haven't added anything worthwhile. Unblemished records, all five of them.'

Henry sat back and looked beseechingly at Mary. 'A small g and t? I need to think and it would help to lubricate my brain.'

Mary laughed. 'You old rogue. You know you can always get round me. Ben, you too?'

'Is that a g and t or can I always get round you? Yes please to both.'

'Let's start with the drink.'

As she was pouring, Henry said, 'So remind me of the plan.'

Ben brought out the blackmail note, written by him with input from MI5. He showed Henry a photo from the clip that would accompany it. It was a still photo from the incriminating video that Stanley Murdock had taken of the conspirators; the same conspirators that were now being murdered in sequence. He read aloud the note that was to accompany the video. 'We know who you are and we know what you and Murdock and Knatchbull were plotting. This information will go to the Chief of the General Staff and some of the more sensational members of the press unless you bring £10,000 to a secure meeting place. If you share this information or do not come alone, any deal will be null and void and you can expect the consequences, You will be given further instructions on the day of the meet.'

He added, 'The second one will be sent the next day and signed by me so he'll know who's blackmailing him. MI5 thought it would be more enticing. It will state that I too will come alone. He'll come armed, of course, and I have to try to get information from him before he's disarmed. We need to know if this really is the end. There's still the other Glasgow killer on the loose. We think he's just a gun for hire but we can't be sure. While he's still out there, we're not out of the woods.'

Mary added, 'We've got Nick's people guarding Chris and Long John but that can't go on for ever.'

Henry rubbed his head. 'Remind me. Nick?'

Ben looked sadly at the old man. This was the first time that Henry had admitted not to be in total command of the facts. 'Nick is the one that got away from the Knatchbull army in reserve – the army which was to be mobilised by an ad in the paper. It was Nick's men who caught Glasgow One.'

Henry sat up. 'Ah yes, the army of malcontents that the regular army spat out. Any more news of attacks on them?'

'No, thank God. With Glasgow One out of the way that seems to have died down.'

Henry said, 'Perhaps he was the leader of the two and the

other one is lying low. How is Knatchbull, by the way? Any improvement?'

'He's surfaced from the induced coma but his memory is shot at the moment. We're hoping it will return but who knows?'

Henry was still looking worried. 'You'll be wearing protective clothing, I hope.'

'I'll have a small gun but I'm sure he'll frisk me and take it from me. That should make him feel safe. And I'll have marksmen all round. Don't worry. He's a General – hasn't fired a shot in anger for many a long year.'

Chapter 31

The silence was deafening. Ben was wired for sound but there was none. MI5 would be recording his exchange with the Enforcer in order to gain evidence and to intervene at the appropriate moment. He looked round the deserted farmyard. Decay was everywhere. Of course he knew that the decay was manufactured but it had been well executed. The farmhouse and barn looked just a little more dilapidated than on his previous visit. The house looked to be better boarded than before but he surmised that entering the house was all part of the MI5 training. The task last time had been to capture Knatchbull. He and Mary had played their parts and since then, Knatchbull had led Ben by circuitous routes to this return visit.

Jeremiah Knatchbull now had memory loss. Ben had been told that intervention had been speedy when Glasgow One had set upon Knatchbull – otherwise he would not have survived. Ben hoped that Knatchbull would be allowed to fulfil his ambitions to go to the opera again and become a Quaker. Ben would certainly suggest this – if they both survived.

He wandered round to the barn and studied it as memories returned. This was where Josephine Finlay had allowed her father to die. This was where it had all begun and, Ben hoped, this was where it would end.

This house, in the dead centre of nowhere, was now an ideal training ground for MI5 and its operatives. In half an hour they would be in place, hidden from view. He would not talk to them today. All had previously been arranged and Ben was confident that their leader, who he was to call 'Midge', knew what to do.

As he approached the barn, he was working out how he could entice the Enforcer inside and where he should position himself to be out of range of cross-fire, if there were to be any. He searched the floor for the speck of ink that had led him to discover the identity of Stanley Murdock's killer. It had long since been washed away. His eyes raked the false back wall and he identified the three small holes where guns would be positioned. His one task was to get information about the present state of the plot to annihilate the Catholic population of Northern Ireland and the plans to systematically kill the plotters and the foot soldiers that the plotters had recruited. And all that without being murdered. He looked at his watch. In one hour he would again be putting himself in the line of fire. He had a lot to live for. He mustn't mess this up.

*　*　*

Ben heard a car in the distance. It stopped further down the lane and no-one arrived at the farmyard. Ben surmised that it must either have been a local farmer or MI5 surveillance. The silence resumed. Not even a bird could be heard and the MI5 operatives hidden in the barn wall, the false chimney and the covered holes in the field were as quiet as the grave. The low hedgerows gave little cover from the chilly East wind blowing across the flat landscape. Ben shivered as he heard the sound of a car. This one slowed as it approached, then turned into the farmyard. The portly figure of General Sir George Crowther-Leakey stepped out and looked around. Ben moved forward to greet him. 'Glad you came. Shall we proceed? Let's move into the barn to get out of this wind.'

'Rather not, old boy. Claustrophobic since Afghanistan. We can talk out here.'

Ben's first line of defence having been removed, he positioned himself and his adversary in line of sight of the snipers in the chimney and those hidden in the adjoining field. Ben replied, 'OK. Suits me. Before we get down to business, do you mind if I ask you a few questions?'

'Feel free. But first, I'll have your gun. I'm sure you have one.'

Ben handed over his gun and allowed himself to be thoroughly frisked. Crowther-Leakey looked at the gun and said, 'Nice. Not army so I wonder where you got it.' As he said this, he tossed Ben's gun into the adjoining field, too far for Ben to have any chance of retrieving it.

Crowther-Leakey continued, 'Now, I'll do a little reconnaissance. I came alone and I need to know that you did too.'

Crowther-Leakey took a small gun from his pocket and

marched over to the house and tried the door. Ben knew that the padlock had been doctored to look dirty and rusty. Crowther-Leakey turned away from the house and walked all round the barn. He stood at the open doors and surveyed the inside. He seemed to Ben to be sniffing the air. He turned to Ben. 'Why do you want the money?'

'It will all go to the charity to help ex-soldiers.'

'Commendable, I'm sure. But you know they're a lost cause. They get warped by what they've seen and done. Irretrievable, all of them.'

Ben wondered if Crowther-Leakey was talking about himself. He knew that he was going to be in conversation with to one of the most malign people he had ever had the misfortune to meet. And, if this quest of his was ever to end, he needed to get answers.

Crowther-Leakey added, 'So what do you want to know?'

The fact that he was happy to talk confirmed for Ben that the conversation would certainly end with bullets. As Ben contemplated his next move, Crowther-Leakey was surveying the farmyard. He added, 'Miserable place, this. I can sense that bad things have happened here.' He pointed to the barn. 'That building is giving off evil vibes.'

Ben was thrown by this remark. How could this man know anything about the deaths – both the suicide of the owner and the killing of Stanley Murdock – that had occurred in that innocuous building. He ignored the remark and asked, 'What will happen to your plot now?'

'Busted, I'm afraid. I'll dispatch the last two conspirators, then hang myself. I've enjoyed keeping to the rhyme. It has memories for me.'

Ben feigned ignorance. 'Rhyme?'

'Ten little soldier boys. You must know it. I worked it up with a chap who died a few years ago, such a sad loss to the cause.'

'Tell me about him.'

'Not important now, but Stanley is much missed. He was my deputy and my soulmate.'

The look in Crowther-Leakey's eyes suggested that Stanley Murdock had meant much more to him than his role as trusted adjutant. He briefly wondered what Murdock's reaction had been but quickly returned to the task in hand.

'Remind me what you have left to do.'

'*Three little Soldier Boys walking in the zoo; A big bear hugged one and then there were two.* I haven't got a big bear but I do have access to fighting dogs so that will suffice.'

Ben looked across at this veteran soldier and wondered what had turned him into what he was now. He realised he was facing a monster with the blandest of countenances. He was speaking to a man who talked as though setting an attack dog on someone was normal. This was a man who, for the sake of a rhyme, had killed and would kill again in the most brutal of ways.

Crowther-Leakey continued, '*Two little Soldier Boys sitting in the sun; One got frizzled up and then there was one.* That will be easy. I'll just make sure he can't escape and then set fire to his house. And last of all, there will be me, *One little Soldier Boy left all alone; He went out and hanged himself and then there were none.* I've been studying Albert Pierrepoint and his methods so I'm content that my death will be relatively painless.'

'Why keep to the rhyme? Why not just kill them the easiest way?'

'Cooked it up with Stanley. It's in memoriam.' He let out a long sigh. 'It's the last thing I have left of him.' Crowther-Leakey suddenly looked bereft. Then he squared his shoulders and asked, 'Any more questions?'

'Yes. What of your two Scottish accomplices?'

'Well, how clever of you. You know about them, then. There's more to you than meets the eye.'

'I was told about old soldiers being killed by men with Scottish accents. I assumed they were something to do with you.' Ben did his best to look confused. 'Have I got that wrong?'

Before answering, Crowther-Leakey pointed to the barn and said, 'I don't like the vibes from that place. I feel that dreadful things have happened there. You don't mind if we move away?' And he grasped Ben's arm and pulled him towards the road. While still holding onto Ben's arm, Crowther-Leakey started walking along the road, back the way he had come and away from the farm. They were still walking away from the farmyard and were now out of the line of sight of all the snipers.

Crowther-Leakey chuckled. He looked, at that moment, like anyone's favourite uncle. 'No, you're not wrong about my Glaswegian accomplices. They weren't accomplices. They were totally under my command.'

Ben now realised he was in extreme danger. He had to keep the other man talking to give the men in black time to regroup. 'Were?' he asked.

'One has disappeared. He's probably dead in a river somewhere. They were both disgusting people. Paedophiles.' Ben could only describe Crowther-Leakey's look as wistful as he added, 'Isn't it dreadful that people transpose homosexuals and paedophiles?' This seemed to have been a rhetorical question as he immediately continued, 'I had a hold over them but I really didn't like dealing with them. Needs must though. I've dispatched the other one. He'd was becoming a liability. He'd reached his sell-by date.'

'You killed him?'

'As I said, he'd become a liability just like the little soldier boys. They had to be disposed of. Had to tidy up the mess. Can't abide loose ends. The army's good like that, teaches you to be tidy.'

At this point Crowther-Leakey looked lovingly at his gun and then pointed it at Ben's heart. He said in a conversational tone, 'It's new issue, a Glock 17 Gen4. A delightful weapon. So light and easy to conceal. It feels good in your hand. Accurate too. If you'd had this in Ireland…' He paused, 'But your wife would still have been killed.'

Ben interrupted this monologue. He had to try to keep Crowther-Leakey talking. 'What about my wife? What do you know?'

'Know a lot about your past. Too late, in many ways. Should have dealt with you in the beginning. And now it's too late for you, old chap. I'm going to have to go. I've got more tidying to do.'

'Please. I need to know.'

Crowther-Leakey looked at his watch. 'A few minutes then. She had to go. We didn't know how she'd rumbled us but she had to be eliminated. We were too late, of course, so we had to regroup and stay operational until those dreadful New Labour people were booted out. Now we find the bloody Libdems are power sharing.'

'But you didn't come after me. Why?'

'Bit of a cock-up that. We knew you were hors de combat with your head injury and nutty as a fruit cake to boot. In the early days we even thought of trying to recruit you into our army. You'd have fitted in with the other nutters. One of our group, Knatchbull I think it was, said you weren't a threat with two brats to bring up, so we let you go. Seems like that was a big mistake. Your one redeeming feature is that you did Stanley proud at his funeral.'

'Stanley Murdock? You were there?'

Ben could see real sadness in his eyes as Crowther-Leakey spoke of Stanley Murdock. 'Couldn't miss it, even though it was dangerous. Slipped in at by a side door with some of our men. Yes, you did him proud, but now it really is time to say goodbye. We've caught up with you at last.'

Crowther-Leakey raised the gun to point at Ben's head. Ben knew that, at this range, there was no hope. He silently thanked Mary for coming into his life. He added a silent goodbye to his family, to Katy, Sarah and his Uncle Mo then he pulled himself up to his full height. He was determined to die like a soldier.

The explosion was earsplitting. Ben found himself on his back in the middle of the road but miraculously he seemed to be alive and unhurt, just deafened. Thank God. MI5 must have got to them in time.

He looked up and was sure that he must be hallucinating. From his prone position, he thought he could see General Craig standing astride Crowther-Leakey's body which was also flat out on the road. He shook his head to clear it and Craig was still there; still pointing his gun at Crowther-Leakey. Ben thought, at first, that Crowther-Leakey must be dead but the groan from the ground confirmed that this was not the case. Crowther-Leakey was holding his gun hand close to his chest. His gun was nowhere to be seen. Craig's gun however was pointed at his heart.

'Get up, you scum. I've only winged you.' Craig gave a hollow laugh. 'And you're right, these new issue Glocks are accurate.' He called out to Ben. 'You OK?'

Ben could not hear the words clearly but assumed their content. He nodded slowly then gingerly raised himself to a sitting position. As he looked around, five men in head-to-toe black ran round the corner with pistols raised. He needed to ensure the status quo. 'Don't shoot,' he shouted and was relieved to see them lower their guns.

In the next minute, they were surrounded by MI5 men. An ambulance appeared from nowhere and, still standing in the road, Crowther-Leakey's hand was examined by a doctor. It was declared to be bruised and the doctor confirmed that he had no other injuries.

At this Craig looked at his gun and said, 'My practice at the shooting range was worthwhile then.' He looked with loathing at his fellow General. 'I needed him to be taken alive.'

Ben shook his head. Thankfully, his hearing was returning. So much so that, as Crowther-Leakey's gun was retrieved by one of the MI5 men and placed in an evidence bag, Ben heard his almost inaudible remark, 'Not that we'll need it.'

Ben introduced General Craig to Midge, explaining he was from MI5. Midge was effusive in his thanks, admitting that they would not have been in time to save Ben. If General Craig agreed, he was to be whisked off with Ben to an MI5 safe house for a debrief. 'Of course.' He turned to Ben. 'I'm sure you'll want to hear the whole story.'

Ben was then checked over. As his blood pressure was being measured he said to Midge, 'Can you contact Parker to ensure that Mary is also present. I'm sure she too wants to know how this man came to save my life.' The doctor admonished him for talking and checked his blood pressure again. Ben was then declared fit to travel.

Crowther-Leakey was hustled, none too gently, into an armoured car. Ben could just see Parker seated in the front. Parker waved to him and gave him a thumbs up. Ben responded in kind. He assumed Crowther-Leakey was to be taken to the facility housing Glasgow One and Knatchbull. No doubt, in due course, he would be told the outcome.

Midge escorted Ben and General Craig to a waiting helicopter and waved them off.

* * *

Ben had no idea where they were going but within ten minutes they were landing at Marshall's Airport in Cambridge. A car then whisked them towards the city centre. They drew up outside a double fronted Victorian house on Maids Causeway. The driver opened the car door and directed them to the black front door. 'Knock just once. I'll go and fetch the young lady.' And he got back in the car and was away.

They did as instructed and the door was immediately opened by a straight-backed man wearing the uniform of a butler. 'This way sirs,' he said as he led the way through the marble hall to a large and sumptuous room at the back of the house. It overlooked a well-kept garden, rather too formal for Ben's taste.

The butler turned to Ben. 'I have been informed that sir might wish to use the facilities. I believe you have some wires to remove.' He handed Ben a small box and gestured for him to follow. Ben was shown into a downstairs shower room with all four walls made of mirrors. He decided it would be best to close his eyes while he removed the bugging devices. He assumed he was to place them in the box. When he emerged, the butler was waiting. He held out a silver tray and Ben placed the box on it. 'Thank you sir. Would you require some refreshment? Your colleague has a glass of the '74 Macallan Malt – a particularly fine example if I may say so.'

As Ben thought he would never again have such an opportunity, he nodded enthusiastically. The butler said, 'We do not advise ice but would sir like a little spring water with it?'

'No, I'll take it neat.'

The butler smiled. 'A very good choice, sir.'

Ben felt as though he had passed some sort of test. He returned to the room and sat opposite General Craig. Craig opened with, 'I think we can now be on first name terms. I'm Walter, by the way, but my friends and family call me Woll.'

'Ben, and my very best friends call me Ben. And now we are out of the noise of the helicopter, I need to thank you again for saving my life. I will be forever in your debt.'

'Not a problem, dear boy. I believe your life to be well worth saving. And I had my own reasons which will become apparent. My problem, at the moment, is how to get my car back from the wilds of Norfolk.'

At that moment, the butler arrived with Ben's drink in a heavy crystal tumbler. He spoke to General Craig. 'Not a problem, sir. If you give me your keys, your car can be delivered to your home – as will you be, in due course.' Keys handed over, the butler departed.

Ben took a sip of the finest whisky he had ever tasted. 'What is this place? Do you know?'

'No idea, no doubt someone will enlighten us in due course. They certainly serve a good whisky. I wonder if dinner is included?'

At that moment, the door opened and a swirl of yellow linen rushed into the room and straight into Ben's arms. 'Thank God you're safe. I knew you would be but I'm so glad to see you in the flesh.' She turned and pointed at General Craig. 'So it wasn't you? You'd be in the dock or the morgue if it were.'

'No, dear lady. It was that bounder Crowther-Leakey but we got him, didn't we, Ben? I think the terminology is "proper banged to rights". It seems this saga is over – I certainly hope so. But you know so much more than I do. I'm assuming your MI5 man will join us soon and then I can tell you my part. Your man will probably not want to share all the story with me but I'll be content if I can be assured that they've all been accounted for.'

Ben's curiosity was piqued. 'I hope he gets here soon. I'm bursting to know what brought you to our meeting place.' He turned to Mary. 'This man saved my life.'

'Then I must give him a hug.' And the embarrassed General Craig was enveloped in a warm embrace.

A voice from the door said, 'Changing your affections, Mrs Amelina? We can't have that.'

Ben decided introductions were in order. 'General Sir Walter Craig, meet Parker.'

Craig laughed. 'Oh, we've met on several occasions. I was always told that he was a "trade ambassador". Never could work out what exactly his role was.' He patted the side of his nose with his forefinger. 'Now I know.'

Parker pressed the bell beside the fireplace and the butler immediately appeared. 'What would everyone like to drink. I think a celebration is in order. Champagne for me. They do a very good Bolly here.' He looked at the assembled company and they nodded assent. 'And bring today's menu, will you?' When the butler had departed, Parker sat down and said, 'I've listened to the recording and it seems that this long and difficult operation is, at last, at an end. All miscreants accounted for. There's still Overton, Thornhill and Asquith left of the original cabal, plus Knatchbull, of course. Thornhill will be the most problematic but I'm sure we can keep him in order.' He turned to General Craig. 'But what we don't know is how you became embroiled – and on the side of the angels.'

General Craig smiled. 'A long story. It all started with my mother. I'm sure you've investigated my background, so you'll know that my family is staunchly Protestant. But my mother fell in love with a Catholic. And not only that, he was from a prominent Republican family. I was the result of that clandestine liaison and she refused to name my father even though her family threatened her. Eventually they backed down and I was accepted into the family. She kept her secret from everyone but me. I knew my father in my childhood. He was a beautiful, gentle man and I loved him dearly. He died when I was twelve. So, you see, I have reason to try to stop a coup that would kill Catholics.'

Parker interrupted, 'But that doesn't tell us how you knew about the plot.'

'That was fortuitous. By happy accident, I went to school with one of the plotters. Geoffrey Asquith is a fellow Wykehamist. We met on our first day. We were new boys together and were both feeling utterly bereft. His father had also died recently. We were two young boys, lonely and lost so we clung to each other. I shared the secret of my paternity with him. We lost touch when we left, but when his fellow plotters began to be murdered, he came to me. He was petrified and asked for my help. I didn't know what to do.' He turned to Ben and Mary, 'And then you two turned up and when you asked about two of the plotters, I knew you were the key. And now the whole bang shoot is wrapped up. At least, I hope it is.'

'Hang on!' said Mary. 'There's still Glasgow Two at large.'

'Ah,' said Parker, 'When you hear the recording of Ben and Crowther-Leakey, you'll know why Glasgow Two has been so quiet recently. Crowther-Leakey killed him. He was tying up all the loose ends before hanging himself. The tenth little soldier boy…'

Mary rejoined with, 'How mad is this man?'

'Oh, at least one box of frogs, possibly two. He'll be on suicide watch until we get what we can from him.'

'And then?'

'Dear lady, you know that it is best not to ask.'

Ben thought he'd better steer away from that subject so said, 'I'd like to talk to you about Knatchbull. It seems he was also party in the past to saving my life.'

Parker replied, 'I'm sure we can accommodate a change in his circumstances. It seems you've led a bit of a charmed life despite some very serious setbacks. You seem to have had several guardian angels. Perhaps now you might consider a short rest from putting yourself in harms way? I think we can safely drink a toast to a job completed. Oh, good. Bolly, my favourite – better than Krug, I think.'

They raised their glasses and Ben silently let out a long sigh.

Parker downed his quickly and said, 'Now, where is that man with the menus? They do a very fine steak and kidney pudding. I do hope they're doing it today.'

The door opened and 'that man' appeared.

Chapter 32

'So Murdock was only the lackey.' Henry laughed heartily. 'I suspect he wasn't at all comfortable in that role. Maybe he had great regard for Crowther-Leakey or, more likely, CL had a hold over him. I wonder what that could have been?'

Mary tapped the old man's arm. 'We'll never know and don't you go looking. We've tied up all the loose ends that need tying. The other ends are doing no harm so they can wave around in the breeze. The conspiracy is dead and, as long as no-one else will be killed, we can rest easy.'

'Yes Ma'am. I'll keep quiet. Ben, shall we have another g and t? You pour. You're more generous than Mary.'

Ben smiled. He knew that their days with Henry were numbered. Although Henry had been energised by his involvement, Ben had seen both a physical and a mental decline in his old friend. In his recent conversations with Henry, he knew that Henry was also tying up loose ends.

Henry raised his glass. 'To a job well done. Now tell me the rest of the gory details.'

'Not gory. Overton has come out of hiding. His death notice was rescinded by saying he'd had an accident and lost his memory. A bit thin but it's difficult to explain away rising from the dead. He's joined with those other two survivors, Thornhill and Asquith, in supporting Chris's venture with ex-soldiers. They're on a jolly in America at the moment to see what the Americans do better than we do. A lot, I think. Apparently, their veterans' associations are quite something. Nick,' Ben had seen a moment of incomprehension. 'You remember Nick? Nick is the rich boy in the East End, one of the recruits to Knatchbull's army of disaffected soldiers. His men caught Glasgow One. Well, he's gone with them. Don't tell them, but he said he fancied a trip to the States and decided that the old farts – his term not mine – needed a chaperone. General Craig, after saving my life, has been up with Chris and Long John nearly every day so I think this charity is going to be big.'

'About time,' said Mary. 'And it's not only ex-army veterans that have been neglected. There are problems with the other services too.'

'And there's good news about Knatchbull. He's making steady progress in his recovery and, as soon as he's well enough, they're going to release him. That's another one who'll rise from the dead. Goodness knows how they'll affect his resurrection. Anyway, I'm going to see him next week and they've given me the task of telling him the good news.'

Henry smiled. 'So he will be able to go to the opera.'

Mary added, 'And join the Quakers.'

'I believe he's a reformed man and I've grown quite fond of him in a funny way. I'm going to miss our sparring matches. But, if they ask me to visit Crowther-Leakey as I did with Knatchbull, I'll refuse point blank.'

Henry said briskly, 'Good man.' Then, in a quieter voice, 'You've done enough in that quarter and I want you to do something for me.'

'Of course,' said Ben. 'What do you want?'

Henry continued, 'I'm not as young as I once was.'

Mary started to remonstrate but Henry waved her to silence. 'Things are hotting up in Ukraine and Crimea will soon be overrun. I don't believe NATO will retaliate so Putin will bide his time and then nibble away at Ukraine's eastern border. Sergei will continue to keep us informed and I want you two to help me to alert our cloth-eared politicians. They don't seem to understand that Putin only understands force. With Putin, diplomacy just won't wash. Will you do that for me, keep on reminding them?'

Ben and Mary looked at each other and then Mary answered for both of them. 'Of course we will, you old duffer.'

'And keep an eye on Sergei? He can be hot-headed at times. He needs calm counsel and you two are just the pair to do it.'

Ben looked at Mary and Mary looked at Ben. Each had a quizzical look as if to say, 'What do you think of that?' Ben knew that Mary was waiting for him to answer. And he also knew that dealing with Mary's ex-husband would not cause him any angst. He responded 'Yes, of course we will.'

Henry pointed to a teetering pile on his desk. 'That's the

important stuff. Evidence that Sergei has garnered inside Russia. Keep it safe.' Henry let out a long breath. 'Now that's done, I can rest easy. Thank you. If you don't mind, I think I'd like to have a little snooze. We'll have another g and t tomorrow eh?'

Chapter 33

'I was never certain. Did you realise that?'

Ben looked at Jeremiah Knatchbull. He was sitting up in his hospital bed looking diminished following his near-death experience. 'No,' Ben answered. 'I never guessed. When you said it to camera, I wasn't sure I believed you. I thought you knew who the Enforcer was and were just stringing me along. Giving me opaque little hints to keep me guessing.'

Knatchbull smiled. 'There was some of that, of course. You were my only conduit to the normality of the outside world. I think I would have gone mad without your visits. I spent the time between those visits preparing for them; sorting out the clues I would give you. I wanted you to come back so I had to feed you breadcrumbs each time.'

'Yeah, you did that all right. Anyway, looking to the future, will you be OK when they let you out?'

'I'm sure they'll make provision to keep me in order. You say they're giving me a new identity. That means I'll be cut off from my former life. I just want to live out the rest of my days quietly. It was true what I said about the Quakers. I want to join – if they'll have me. One sinner who repents, etc. If the powers will let me leave the country, I'd like to visit some Shaker places in New England. I'm sure they'll let me resume my opera visits, and I'm glad you said I'll be recompensed for the disposal of my assets. I don't know what I'd have done otherwise. I should have enough to get by.'

'You've been incarcerated and beaten to within an inch of your life. Aren't you at all bitter?'

'No. That would be a complete waste of energy. And anyway, I was part of an evil plot, I got caught out by a very clever adversary and I got my just desserts. Even the beating, that was because I was too confident of my abilities and I paid the price. So, the next time I deal with a psychopath, I'll be more careful.'

'Let's hope you don't meet any more. Tell me, what did you

say to make him attack you?'

'It was ridiculous really. I stupidly asked him about Rangers and Celtic. He thought I was implying that there was a comparison to be made and, in his mind, there is none. To him, there's no equivalence – not in the same league – even if in reality, they are. I mentioned the two in the same sentence and that was enough for him to want to beat me to a pulp.' Knatchbull gave a grim smile. 'Football eh? Bill Shankley was right. To some people it is more important than life and death. Unfortunately, I met one of those.'

'But fortunately, you have survived. I think your beating may have tipped the balance towards your release. When you get out, will you ever go back to Ireland? You've got history there.'

'If they'll let me. I want to go back to the start of my radicalisation. I want to make a pilgrimage and throw white flowers into the sea where Louis and Nicholas were killed – and that other poor boy. Do you think they'll let me?'

Ben replied, 'I'll put in a word for you. At the moment I'm a blue-eyed boy so I think they'll listen.'

'Thank you. That's much appreciated. And my prison will still presumably have two inmates. The Glasgow psychopath and Crowther-Leakey. Is he a psychopath, do you think?'

'Could be a sociopath. Who knows?'

'Do you think they'll manage to crack either of them?'

Ben thought for a moment. 'I think they'll have a damn good try. They need to understand what they can do to stop radicalisation and subsequent terrorism. Whether they'll be successful with either of them, I have my doubts. Have you offered to help? Not with those two, of course, but more generally. I think Parker would accept your assistance. After all, you've seen it from the other side.'

'I haven't offered but it's a good idea. But do you think radicalisation is the same for all ethnic groups?'

Ben nodded. 'Some similarities, I'm sure. Different religious or political bases but there must surely be similar triggers. I'm sure they could learn from you. And, if you offer, it will give you Brownie points if nothing else.'

'I'll do that. Can you pass the message on for me?' Knatchbull grasped Ben's arm with a strength that belied his frail appearance. 'And Ben, will you keep visiting me. I think I will not have many friends.'

Chapter 34

27th February 2014

Ben and Mary were sitting companionably together in the warm kitchen sipping strong black coffee. After a full week's rest and recuperation together Mary had suggested that they were now ready to meet the world.

'Who shall we visit first? We should go to Brighton and see Allie and Ginny. She tells me she's showing quite well now and the babies are really beginning to wriggle. I'd just love to feel them moving.'

Ben agreed. 'Twins, yeah. We'd better visit before she gets to the stage of having difficulty getting around. I remember… '

'Go on. You were going to say something about Diane.'

'Katy was a big baby. Diane used to say she knew what a beached whale feels like.'

Mary clasped Ben's hand and silently kissed his cheek.

Ben continued, 'I'm very lucky. I've had two exceptional women in my life. Yes. Very, very lucky.'

They sat in silence for a moment, each deep in their own thoughts. Then Mary lightened the mood with, 'Yes, you've had two spies, a murderer and Detective Chief Inspector. Quite a haul – and that's only the ones I know about!'

Ben corrected her. 'Only technically a murderer – and technically the case is still open. And you and I both know that the Josephine of today is not the Josephine who allowed Stanley Murdock to die. Did I tell you she's volunteering at Citizen's Advice? Her background in the law will be a huge asset.'

'And Agnes and Mo are so busy with the U3A that we'll have to book a slot for a visit. We'll have to wrap up warm for that one. Hunny in February will be freezing.'

'For Brighton maybe we could coincide with one of Tommy's visits. He'll make such a wonderful grandfather. I've been wondering for a while if he'll move here. I don't think there's anyone to keep him in Moira. And the pull of grandchildren must be very strong.'

'Especially for Tommy.'

'And Vin's wedding's coming up. Getting entangled with me doesn't seem to have had a detrimental effect on her love life or her prospects of promotion.'

Mary smiled and Ben's heart lurched as she said, 'Getting entangled with you was the best thing I ever did.' Then she brought them back to visits. 'Chris and Long John must be high on the list. I'm dying to see what progress they've made. They've even got the local MP involved.'

'Cynical maybe, but I'm sure it won't hurt their chances of re-election.'

'Anyone else?'

'I must catch up with Alison. Now she's officially signed me off, I've got to go and thank her for keeping me reasonably sane for all these years. And Knatchbull, of course. He'll need me for a while, until he gets some Quaker friends.'

'But your two beautiful daughters must come first. Katy's washing brings her here regularly but you haven't seen Sarah since Christmas. I wonder if she and Dani will get married when it becomes legal. Hope so – then you can be father of one of the brides. And we must set a date for our wedding.'

'Lots to keep us occupied.' Ben looked at his watch. 'Time for the news.' He turned on the radio.

A serious voice intoned, 'After several days of unrest, a large contingent of heavily armed men have seized and occupied the Crimea Parliament Building. It is understood that, during the occupation, and behind closed doors, the parliament has voted to terminate the Crimean Government, replace the Prime Minister and to hold a referendum on greater autonomy on the 25th of May.'

Ben and Mary looked at each other. 'It's begun.'

Book 4 - Bury the Past

is the last in this series. So, what next?

Worlds Apart

I plan to return to an idea I first had in 2014. What if, in an alternative universe, George Washington did not dodge the bullet that nearly killed him and, in consequence, a leaderless America lost the war of independence? In this alternative reality, the world would be a structurally different place. It is probable that Britain would reign supreme. In this scenario, would there have been two world wars? And, if not, would there have been the same imperative to create a state of Israel? I've created people in the past but never a whole world. Will it be worse or better than the one we live in? Dystopian or utopian? Who knows? Oh, what fun!

The three preceding books in this series:

Book 1 – Bury the Truth

He's riddled with guilt about his wife's death. He couldn't save her so he must save others, even a murderer – especially this murderer.

June 2012

Stanley Murdock's corpse arrives in Ben's mortuary- and everything changes. For Ben, it is imperative that he finds Stanley's killer before anyone else does. His sanity depends on it.

Stanley had a secret life and many enemies. Even his own children hated him – but was it enough to kill him?

Book 2 - Bury the Lies

He removes evidence from a murder scene. He has people he needs to protect. When he is targeted and his family threatened, he decides to become the bait to catch the killer.

November 2012

Ben Burton receives an anguished message from Professor Dobson at St Etheldreda's College. He discovers Dobson's body in his ransacked rooms. Ben believes that Dobson was a blackmailer and removes a list of names. Then he calls the police.

DCI Vin Wainright and her team arrive. Ben is sleeping with Vin and she is his alibi for the time of the murder. He has not told her that he and Dobson both worked for MI5. He contacts Chris, his handler. Chris organises for Ben's firm to bury Dobson as cover for investigating his death.

Ben's world is rocked when he finds clues about his wife's death among Dobson's effects.

Then a nun is murdered…

Book 3 - Bury the Pain

Only by returning to Northern Ireland and finding the truth about his wife's death can he gain peace of mind. But, in finding his own peace, he uncovers a plot which could destroy the fragile peace in Northern Ireland.

February 2013

Ben Burton is recovering from a complete breakdown caused by finding evidence of his wife's double life. He discovers an old photo from their time in Northern Ireland but can't remember who took it. He finds a coded message. 'Find Moira then find Kevin's cousin. You'll know him when you see him.' He sets out to crack the code.

He uncovers evidence that Stanley Murdock and Jeremiah Knatchbull, a mid-ranking MI5 officer led a plot to commit genocide in Northern Ireland and that plot is still ongoing. Knatchbull has now risen to second tier MI5.

Ben must seek him out and outwit this powerful adversary …

Printed in Great Britain
by Amazon